Listening for Crickets

Listening for Crickets

DAVID GIFALDI

HENRY HOLT AND COMPANY
NEW YORK

Chapter One

ONE OF MY best dreams ever. A flying dream. Me, Jake Wasniewski, with wings like a megabat, a flying fox. Powerful wings. Only these aren't brown. They're blue. And sparkly. A single stroke shoots me into an updraft, my stomach racing to keep up. Farms and rivers slide by. Up ahead, a city of glass, shining like a treasure in the sun. Then . . . voices. My bat ears twitch. *Huh?*

They're at it again. Smack in the middle of my flying dream. I check the clock on the nightstand, the green numbers ghosting 11:35. The back-and-forth words coming from the kitchen get louder, sharper.

Wish our house had an upstairs like Luke's.

Wish I had a remote control that could mute anything.

"Jake," Cassie murmurs.

"It's okay," I say, reaching to flick on the lamp.

Cassie squints even though the yellow light is dim. She listens to the harsh-sounding words, then rolls out of bed, Thumper tucked safely under one arm.

Scampering around to the bed's other side, she squeezes between mattress and wall, and pushes, grunts. The bed moans, then gives in to be scraped across the floor. Cassie pushes—grunts—until the mattress bumps the nightstand. She knows that's as far as she can go.

"You can't be moving your bed right up to mine," I've had to tell her more than once. "See that night-stand there? . . . That's the limit. That's the boundary. That whole strip there is poison. It's bad enough we have to share the same room, bad enough you get scared. A guy needs his privacy."

She smiles over at me, that goofy seven-year-old

grin of hers, then bounds up onto the mattress, slithers under the sheet, moves Thumper up top for air, and sighs. "You can turn the light off now."

"Oh, can I?" I say, a little mad at the bossy sound of her voice, as if a soon-to-be second grader could ever tell a soon-to-be fifth grader what to do.

I reach over and flick off the lamp. Mom and Dad are flinging spears at each other. *I'm selfish? Look who's talking. Me? Don't make me laugh! You don't have a clue, do you? . . .*

"Okay, Jake," Cassie says through the new dark.

That means it's time for another story. Sometimes I wish I hadn't started this whole story thing. As if telling stories to your little sister could ever cover up the arguing.

"You'd better be listening," I say, "because I'm starting right now and the last time you didn't hear the beginning because you were listening to something else. You hear?"

"Uh-huh."

Suddenly the back-and-forth spears stop. Hard

footsteps. The front door slamming—so hard the whole house jumps, including my ears. Lights swing past the window as the car backs onto the street. I wait till I can't hear the engine anymore. Then the kitchen screen door opens and slams, and I know Mom is outside fumbling for a cigarette.

"Jake?"

"Dang it, Cassie. Hold your horses."

I cross my hands behind my head, slide my feet beneath the sheet to find some fresh cool. At least I won't have to talk loud.

"Once," I begin. "Once there was a baby dragon named Smoke. A girl dragon. And she had a brother dragon named Bonfire. And the two liked to stomp over the world and play all the latest dragon games . . . like . . ."

"Like what?" Cassie says, unable to stop herself. There's real interest in her voice, and I can tell she's glad too that the shouting has stopped.

"I'm thinking," I say.

"Don't rush Jake, Thumper," she says, as if I

might actually fall for a talking stuffed rabbit. "It's his story and he'll tell it the way he wants. . . . Right, Jake?"

I draw circles with my toes under the sheet and go on, telling whatever comes to mind, about Smoke and Bonfire, about their life in a tiny cave on the side of a mountain, how the two are learning to fly, how Bonfire did his first loop-de-loop today, how Smoke got so excited she torched one of the trees outside the cave.

I keep talking until Cassie's even breathing lets me know she's asleep. I listen hard for wheezing, but her air sounds clear. Then Mom taps at the door and steps in, a strip of living-room light cutting across my bed.

"You kids okay?"

I don't say anything.

She moves to our beds, checks Cassie, sees the bed has been moved again.

"She okay?" she asks, cigarette smell moving over me.

"Yeah," I answer.

I turn over just as she leans down to kiss me, turn quickly so I won't have to see if she's been crying.

"Good night, then," she whispers.

" 'Night," I say into my pillow, thinking of where I want the new dragon story to go . . . how next time maybe Smoke and Bonfire will leave their tiny cave for a bigger and better one . . . one with room after room after room, high up on the tallest mountain, where the air is so clean you can breathe it all the way down to your toes and not wheeze or cough.

The clock shows 12:00. Midnight. I close my eyes and reach for my wings.

Chapter Two

THE NEXT MORNING I stay in bed till Dad leaves for work. When I come out, Mom looks tired. "Hurry, Jake!" Cassie says around a mouthful of Frosted Flakes. "We're gonna get our school stuff."

The three of us take the bus to Wal-Mart. The school-supplies aisle is mobbed with kids and parents stuffing carts and baskets.

"Fifteen and twenty . . . including backpacks . . . not a penny over," Mom says for the second time. That means Cassie gets to spend fifteen dollars and I get twenty.

"O-*kay*," I say, doing a quick check to see if I recognize any kids from school or the park pool. I hate Mom's talk about money and how we don't have enough.

It's hard not to get excited about all the fancy new binders, folders, markers, packs, and things. I end up with a decent backpack, a binder, paper, colored pencils, and a zippered pouch decorated with a cool-looking alien whose eyeballs sling down to his knees. "*Ewww!*" the clerk says when she rings it up, which makes me know I made the right choice.

Cassie won't even let the cashier put her Barbie backpack in a bag. The pack is pink with a yellow-haired Barbie and purple zippers and pockets. She hugs it all the way to the bus stop.

We hardly have to wait before the bus pulls up.

"In four days I'll be a second grader," Cassie tells the driver. The man smiles, like it's something he's been waiting all his life to know.

The air inside the bus is hot and stuffy. Cassie chooses a seat toward the back, and Mom and I take the one behind her. Cassie coughs, once, then goes back to humming and fiddling with the zippers on her new pack.

Mom looks out the window, but I don't think she's seeing the things passing by. She still looks tired. I think about the yelling last night and how Mom and Dad seem to fight all the time now.

"Is Dad starting on a new house today?" I say. Usually I can tell how a fight ended by how Mom acts when I mention Dad. But Mom's not talking. She just shrugs, her eyes still staring out the smudged-up window.

Dad's newest job is painting houses. He used to work at Jiffy Lube, but he was let go because he told his boss to kiss his exhaust pipe. Before that he drove a vegetable truck. And before that he worked for a company that does blacktopping. Dad says it's the pits working at one *shitty* job after another. 'Course if I used that word, I'd get my mouth washed out with soap.

The bus passes a 7-Eleven, and Mom snaps out of her staring. "After the first week, you kids'll have to get yourselves off to school on time," she says. "Your father and I'll both be gone."

Mom's gonna start a new job working part-time at the 7-Eleven across from Safeway. She says walking the seven blocks to work will help her lose weight. She hasn't worked since the Fresh Breeze Laundromat got sold and became Scrub-A-Dub-Dog, sort of a car wash for dogs.

"I'm getting all pluses this year," Cassie turns to say. "I made up my mind."

"Yeah, sure," I say. But it makes me think. For the first time ever I'm looking forward to school. Mrs. Maw said in June that this was going to be my year. "Like the Chinese New Year," she said. "But instead the Year of the Snake, it'll be the Year of the Jake."

Mrs. Maw likes to joke a lot, which is a good thing because she's got a hard job teaching us Low Expectation kids. She's our school's LEP teacher. LEP means Learning Enrichment Program. But everybody knows it's for dummies like me.

Later I ride over to Luke's and pick him up for swimming. Once I cross Fremont Street, it's a breeze. The sidewalks are wide and smooth, and the trees block the sun. Luke is already on his bike when I get there, tracing figure eights in the driveway. We streak for the park, then stand in line outside Vista Park Pool, waiting for the doors to open. Luke's shorter than me. His hair's the color of straw. It flops over his ears. Earlier in the summer he told me his parents were thinking about splitting up. I ask him about it.

"That's when they were calling each other names and fighting all the time," he says. "They don't fight that much anymore. They've been paying money to some guy who shows them how to be nice to each other again."

"You can do that?"

"Yeah, a mental counselor guy . . . a psycho or something."

"How much is it?" I say.

"Beats me."

"Like, a *lot*?"

He shrugs. "Maybe. Dad said we couldn't afford to go on vacation this summer."

Luke and I come to the outdoor pool almost every afternoon. We get to ride our bikes and be on our own as long as we stay together. When it's really hot and Cassie feels okay, Mom and her walk to the pool. Sometimes they pick up Luke's little sister, Erin, and Luke's mom, who's the thinnest lady I've ever seen. Luke says his mom eats more than anyone in the family, but she never gains an ounce. When my mom and Luke's mom are together, they look like an advertisement for a weight-loss company—Mom is *Before* and Mrs. Gilliam is *After*.

Luke is my age. We're in the same Cub Scout den. I wish he went to Marshall Elementary with me, but he goes to St. Joe's instead. He's really smart. He can tell you facts about stuff you never thought of. Like the number of times a hummingbird beats its wings every second (seventy-five). And how much time the average person has spent eating by the end of his life (four and a half years). He also knows that dolphins sleep with one eye open, and a giraffe's tongue is almost two feet long. I like him because he thinks my webbed toes are cool and because his parents yell at each other too.

The kids who are barefoot keep running onto the grass for relief. Someone up ahead in line starts making hand-in-the-armpit farts. Soon everybody's doing it. The wet under my arm makes mine sound squishy. "Cool," Luke says, working for the same sound. We look like one-armed chickens trying to fly.

Two lifeguards come out when it's time. They're both tan. The girl has a red bathing suit with a towel wrapped around her waist. The guy wears a red Speedo and a pair of yellow flip-flops. You can tell he's proud of his body. You can also tell some of the kids are embarrassed for him. A few girls snicker.

"You guys line up single file and have your quarters ready," he says.

"And no pushing!" the girl says, retying her ponytail. She could be a movie star. Most of the older boys can't take their eyes off her.

The thing about my family is, other than Cassie, we're not all that much to look at. It's not that we'd be mistaken for a family of rhinos or anything. It's just that Dad has bad teeth, Mom is overweight, and I have stick-out ears and webbed toes. How I got webbed toes is a mystery. Mom doesn't have them. Neither does Dad. And they can't remember anyone in their families talking about webbed toes. "Most of my family can't even swim," Mom says.

Luke and I push along with everyone else into the men's locker room. There's lots of noise as shirts and shorts go flying in a dash to be first in the water.

"Not so fast!" the red-suited lifeguard says at the pool entrance. "You guys know you have to shower."

The shower room has nozzles sticking out along three walls. Luke and I share a nozzle, mostly standing back and letting the water bounce off our palms. The water is freezing cold. It makes our arms break out in goose bumps.

Luke looks down at my feet. He has to look every time. "I still think it's a lucky mark," he says. "Like Harry Potter's lightning bolt. Maybe it's magic. Maybe you were chosen for something special."

I give him an elbow. He wobbles forward to keep his balance, and gasps, the cold water pelting his head. That shuts him up. I know he's not making fun of me, but the last thing I need is another mob of guys gawking at my toes.

As far as I know there's nothing magical or special about the second and third toes of both my feet being nearly all-the-way joined by skin that shouldn't be there. Weird, maybe. But not magical. The thing is, it's really not that noticeable. I hardly thought about it myself until last year when fourth grade went to the middle school for swim lessons.

That's when Matt Horvath screamed to the whole locker room, "Hey, look at *this!*"

Suddenly I was a human magnet, all these chlorine-smelling guys in their wet underwear racing over to stare at my feet.

"Weird."

"Gross."

"Wow!"

"Yuck."

"Hey, Jake's part frog!"

"Ribbet!" this big kid, Daniel, said. "Ribbet! Ribbet! Ribbet!"

This was the same kid I'd felt sorry for earlier when one of the guys called him a whale. *Traitor!* I ran at him, pushing him against the lockers. He let out an *oomph* and reached for his side. "Ow!" he said. "My appendix! You frog." His eyes were little slits. He pushed me hard in the chest, causing me to fall over the bench behind me. "Whale!" I said.

Next thing I knew we were rolling, wrestling, the floor and our bodies too wet for either of us to get a good hold.

"Fight . . . fight!" someone shouted out the locker-room door.

"What's going on in there?" Mrs. Sinclair yelled.

"Jake broke Daniel's appendix and Daniel's trying to squash Jake!"

"I told you not to goof around in there. Now cover yourselves, I'm coming in!"

She did too, bursting through the doorway like the first firefighter at the scene of a fire. I had to sit on a bench beside Mrs. Sinclair for the last two days of swim lessons, sweating in my clothes and watching everyone else have a good time. Luke says keeping a guy with webbed toes from swimming is cruel punishment and that a good lawyer could have gotten me off.

We stay in the pool until time is up and the lifeguards blow their whistles and yell at everybody to get out. The locker room reeks of chlorine and wet socks. Almost every kid has red eyes.

"Aliens have landed," I tell Luke.

"Sunburned, butt-naked aliens," he says.

We burst out laughing and keep laughing the whole time we're dressing. Whenever one of us calms down a little, the other says *butt-naked aliens,* and we go crazy again. That's the way it is with me and Luke. We get these laughing fits.

Chapter Three

DAD IS HOME from work when I get back to the house. He's on his knees in front of the garage in his paint-spotted coveralls, the lawn mower upside down in front of him. He's using a putty knife to knock off old clumps of hardened grass from the mower. He stops when he sees me, uses a rag to wipe his forehead, then sips the beer beside him.

"Honey!" he yells toward the back door. "Here he is."

Honey? That means they've made up.

Mom looks out. "Where've you been? The afternoon swim closes at four."

"Four thirty, Mom. . . . I've told you a million times. Where's Cassie?"

"She's watching that show she likes. She took her medicine and ran through the sprinklers for a while."

Connected to the side of the garage is a tiny wooden shed. Dad keeps shovels and rakes and stuff there. That's where I go to change into my cat clothes . . . the clothes I wear when I go to Mrs. Pittmon's. I can't keep them inside our house because the hair and dander from Mrs. Pittmon's cats can trigger Cassie's asthma.

I change quickly, taking my cat clothes out of the black garbage bag and putting my un-cat clothes in the clear one. Dad's using a wrench to take the blade off the mower when I get back out front. "Surprised the thing cuts at all," he says, standing up with the blade in hand. "When are you gonna learn how to do stuff like this?"

"I don't know," I say.

"Well, you're old enough."

I don't mention that he told me never to start up the mower without him. And that the last time I touched one of his tools I was grounded for a week. And that usually when I work with him he gets all upset and says he should have known better. He takes another sip of the beer and sets it back down.

"I'm about to sharpen the blade if you want to watch."

"I should get over to Mrs. Pittmon's," I say. "She's expecting me."

"Suit yourself," he says.

I feel funny about leaving. I know he'd like me to stay. He'd probably even let me do some of the sharpening. But if I make a mistake . . . what then? He'd get mad for sure. He's been getting mad a lot lately.

Mrs. Pittmon lives next door, on the other side of a thick hedge. Her house is just like ours. Dad says the two houses were built a long time ago by some guy who wanted to make as much money as possible.

The guy built the littlest houses he could, squeezing two into a space that was made for one.

"About time," Mrs. Pittmon says when I bound onto her front porch. She's waiting just behind the screen door in her wheelchair. She wheels herself back, clearing the door for me. I step up and in, my nose wrinkling in self-defense, the way it's learned to do. But today something besides cats is in the air. Something good, sweet.

She rolls the chair a few inches forward, so I'm kind of trapped there in front of the door. She's pretty old, her hair white as snow, but there's nothing weak about her voice. "You tell your mom and dad to shut the windows over there the next time they have a row. A good Christian woman like me don't wanna hear no such trash in the middle of the night. . . ."

She stops. I think she's going to say something about calling the cops next time, but she doesn't. She's always threatening to call the cops about things she doesn't like in the neighborhood.

"Well, better stop wasting time. Get yourself in here and march to the kitchen. I made some of them cookies you like."

On the low, specially built counter in the kitchen is a sheet of cookies, each cookie jammed full of chocolate chips. My mouth jets water. I'm plain starving from swimming. I grab two and look around for Otto and Nina.

"Oh, they're here," she says. "Another hard day at the office for those two . . . moving from one cushion to the next." She points to the cookies in my hand. "Good?"

"Really good," I say.

"You told me you like them almost raw."

Actually, it's Cassie who likes her cookies raw. I like mine a little crispy. Mrs. P. gets things turned around sometimes.

"I got a new bag of litter," she says. "Ordered a twenty-five pounder. So you can throw out everything that's there."

I finish off the second cookie, thankful that I

don't have to sift through Nina and Otto's box for turds today.

Since the two houses are identical, Nina and Otto have the same room that me and Cassie have . . . the smaller bedroom off the living room. Mrs. P. calls it the cats' room. I call it *The Bead Room,* because it has a curtain of beads instead of a door. I like how the beads give way when you go through, rustling as they brush across your skin.

Today Nina is coiled on the old sofa. Otto is spread out on the wood floor, full in the sun coming through the window. They push themselves up and stretch when they see me, knowing it's feeding time.

Mrs. P. keeps all her old plastic bags in The Bead Room's closet. I pull out the biggest one I can find and dump the cat-box litter into it, jerking my head out of the way of the dust and pee smell.

"You guys should be ashamed of yourselves," I tell them as the dust settles. "All you have to do is go outside once in a while and do your duty there."

They don't care. Nina's still on the sofa, licking

her gray fur. Otto has hopped onto the back of the chair nearest the window. He's almost a perfect match for the chair's rusty orange material. The extra toe on each front foot makes his feet look like a lion's. He leaps to follow me when I take the box outside to hose it down.

Suddenly, my ears twitch. I let up on the spray nozzle and listen. I can't tell if Dad's yelling at the mower, or if he's talking loud so Mom can hear him through the back door. My stomach feels funny, like maybe I ate the cookies too fast.

Back inside, I hurry to clean out the cats' bowls and split a can of food between them. I change their water too. Mrs. P. wheels herself from the stove to the counter where her purse is. She hands me a dollar.

"You're a godsend," she says, pointing to a fat square of foil on the counter, which I know has cookies in it. "Make sure your sister gets some."

I leap off the porch and hurry around the hedge to our driveway. The mower is still apart on the ground. But the car is gone. Dad must have needed something at the hardware store. Inside, the TV is so loud the kitchen floor is thumping. Envelopes and pieces of paper are scattered all over the place. I peek into the living room. *Road Runner*'s on.

"Mom? Cassie?"

I run to our room. Cassie's there on the bed.

"What?" I say. "Where's Mom and Dad? . . . Why you cryin'?"

"Mom opened the mail," she says, her shoulders moving like she's got the hiccups. ". . . And there were bills and Mom yelled because Dad bought lottery tickets again and Dad got mad and threw the tickets and Mom started crying and said she was going for a walk and Dad got in the car and left. He said bad words."

She sniffs up some of the wet running down her upper lip, and has to reach for her next breath. "I tried to make them stop."

"Turning up the TV won't make them stop," I say. "I told you that a hundred times." I hand her a tissue from the box on the nightstand. "You'd better calm down or you're gonna make yourself sick."

The TV's sound is still throbbing through the floorboards. I run to the living room to turn it off. Grabbing the remote, I stop. Wile E. Coyote is rolling a bomb into Road Runner's hole. Road Runner escapes out the back and hands Wile E. the bomb with its fizzing wick, then spins his legs into a blur and *beep-beeps* away. Wile E. reaches back to throw the bomb after him. I press Off just as the screen fills with smoke. Serve 'em right if they both blow up.

Chapter Four

CASSIE'S COUGHING. Prob'ly 'cause I came into the house with my cat clothes on. Mom makes her use the inhaler and tells me to take a shower to get the cat stuff off me before bed.

I take my pajamas into the bathroom, slipping past Dad, who sits at the table with the paper and a small plastic cup. I'm thinking this might be the cleanest I've ever been in my life—two hours of swimming and now a shower on the same day. When I get dressed, I brush my teeth in front of the mirror. I brush hard, not wanting my teeth to get like

Dad's. I spit and rinse and show my teeth to the mirror. Not bad. My hair's gotten long again over the summer. I flick the sides back and take a look at my stick-out ears. Bat ears. They're like bookends evenly placed on either side of my head. They make me look like I'm always listening.

"Done," I say to Mom after hurrying through the kitchen.

She's sitting in the living room watching some lawyer show on TV. She waves me over for a hug. Her hair smells a little of the refried beans we had for supper. I start back toward the bedroom, but she makes a noise, and when I turn around she's pointing to the kitchen. *Do I have to?* I mouth. She nods.

I go to the doorway and poke my head in. Dad's checking the want ads, head cocked toward the Mariners game on the radio. "G'night," I say.

He turns down the radio. "Come and give your ole dad a hug."

I take a step back. I don't mean to, it just happens.

Even from where I stand I can smell the whiskey on his breath, the cigarette smoke on his clothes.

He taps his leg. "You're not too old to sit on your ole man's lap, are you?"

It's more ordering than asking. He pushes the chair away from the table and pulls me onto his lap where the cigarette smell is stronger. Then he hooks his arm around me and leans into me so that his whiskers scrape my cheek, causing the tiny hairs on the back of my neck to stand up.

"You're growing so fast," he says. "You and Cassie both. . . . I thought we'd be in a better place by now."

He stares across the table at the photo on the wall. The picture shows the four of us, two summers ago, when we went to Oaks Park and spent the whole day on rides and playing games. SOUVENIR OF OAKS PARK is printed across the bottom. Cassie's named the stuffed rabbit Dad won for her Thumper even before we'd left the park.

In the picture I look goofy, my cap on sideways. Dad has one arm around Mom and one around me.

He's smiling all the way across his face, but the camera's far enough away so his teeth don't look bad.

Dad turns from the photo and I feel another whisker scrape. "How 'bout you and me taking in a Seahawks game this fall? Just us two."

Matt and David went to a Seahawks game last year with their dads. They took the train. Matt said they ran back and forth through the cars for three hours, buying snacks. They talked about the trip for days after and got to share pennants and mini footballs in front of the class.

"We could take the train," I tell Dad. "It goes right to the stadium. You wouldn't have to find a parking place."

He nods. "We'll see. Go to bed now. Try not to wake your sister."

I walk past Mom (who gives me a thumbs-up) and tiptoe into the bedroom, closing the door as softly as I can. The light from the street makes it easy to see where things are. I'm about to reach my bed when I hear "Jake? . . . Is that you?"

"Cassie, you know dang well it's me."

"I couldn't see for sure."

I pull the covers down and slip in.

"Is Daddy still here?"

" 'Course he's still here. He's in the kitchen reading the paper."

She doesn't say anything. I fold my hands behind my head. Outside, a car goes by with music blaring. I hear Cassie moving under the covers in her bed, but I don't take my eyes off the ceiling.

"Is Mommy still here?"

"Cassie, Mom is sitting right out there not fifteen feet away behind that door. Can't you hear the TV?"

You'd think she'd stop being so afraid. Every time Mom and Dad have a blowout, Cassie thinks Dad will leave or Mom will leave or the whole world will leave or blow up or something crazy like that.

"You don't have to worry," I say. "Mom'll be starting at the 7-Eleven, so she won't need to get upset about bills anymore. Everything'll be all right."

Everything'll be all right. But it never gets right. Not really. Just a little right here and a little right there. And in between are the wrongs: the yelling and swear words and slamming doors.

"Jake?"

"Go to sleep, Cassie."

Maybe that will do it. That's what I need to do, get forceful about it. Let her know who's boss. If she goes to sleep right away I won't have to make up a story tonight. One story after another. It's like Cassie thinks I'm a writer or a storyteller or something. I'm just dumb Jake, for cryin' out loud.

"Smoke is all upset," she says.

"What?"

"Smoke . . . from last time. You said she was stuck in the cave. She'd landed wrong on her foot when she flew into the cave for shelter. And she broke her ankle. That's what you said."

I keep looking at the ceiling. "She didn't *break* her ankle. She *turned* it. There's a big difference. And Smoke doesn't need to get all upset, because Bonfire is on his way with Dr. Scorch, the dragons' top doctor."

"Why does she need a doctor if her ankle isn't broke?"

" 'Cause it's swollen. And it might get infected. So Dr. Scorch is flying in to give her some medicine. She has to take the medicine twice a day. And it tastes horrible, but it's really good for her."

"How horrible?"

"What?"

"How horrible does the medicine taste?"

"It's made from gopher guts and fish eyes, if you must know."

(Good one. I actually hear her shiver.)

"Then suddenly," I say, "there's this wonderful music playing. You can hear it all over the canyon, even up in Smoke and Bonfire's cave. It sounds like crickets chirping . . . a million crickets all together. And it goes like this: *chirr—chirr—chirchirchir.*

"Dr. Scorch says it *is* crickets. It's the Cricket Choir. They only sing when things are going to be all right. He says you only need to worry when there isn't any music . . . that the worst thing is when the crickets go silent. That means the Beastie-Beasts are about."

"Beastie-Beasts, Jake? What are Beastie-Beasts? You never said there were Beastie-Beasts."

"Because they weren't in the story yet," I say. "Will you let me finish?"

"Okay."

". . . Anyway, Smoke says she's glad there's a Cricket Choir tonight. She was kind of worried about Beastie-Beasts because of her ankle. Then Bonfire and Smoke say good-bye to Dr. Scorch; he's got to fly home before dark because he's getting old like Mrs. Pittmon and his eyes aren't as good as they used to be.

"Then Bonfire makes Smoke swallow her medicine."

(Cassie's tongue clicks the roof of her mouth.)

". . . And tells her to get her sleep because tomorrow they'll be flying to the Kingdom of Bats, where they'll meet the Bat King himself, who might have the answer for saving the whole realm from the evil Beastie-Beasts."

I need a big breath after all that.

"The end," I say. "Now go to sleep."

Cassie doesn't say anything, just rolls over.

I'm wondering what the heck Beastie-Beasts are when I hear the TV go off and see the strip of light underneath the door disappear. Footsteps. Floorboards creaking. Toilet flushing. Water running. Door closing.

. . . All right.

I turn off my bat ears and go to sleep.

Chapter Five

I WAKE UP with the idea. A cave. Like Smoke and Bonfire's. Cassie and I spend the whole morning building it.

"It'll be a place only we know about," I say. "You can't tell Mom or Dad or anyone. You hear?"

"Right," she says. "Just for us."

We're at the back of the hedge that separates our backyard from Mrs. Pittmon's. Here the hedge is almost as high as the houses. Dad calls the hedge *the monster.* He gave up a long time ago trying to keep *the monster* trimmed. He figures if the guy who owns our house doesn't care if the hedge takes over the yard, why should he.

I use Dad's pruning saw and Mom's rose snippers to cut. I'm like a surgeon, called in special for the job. I have to cut out the hedge's insides without disturbing the outside walls and ceiling.

"Nina and Otto know about the hedge," I say, pushing out another branch for Cassie to heap on the pile on the grass. "Once when it was raining I couldn't find them. I went out back with a can of food and tapped the can with a spoon. And the both of 'em came running outta the hedge, dry as could be. Later I went to see where they'd been. They had a place—a safe place—right in the middle of the hedge. You'd never find it if you didn't know. The hedge is so thick, even the rain can't get through. And a dog could never squeeze through all these branches."

Now that I've got a good start, I call Cassie in. She grunts, holding aside the two big leafy limbs that form the outermost layer, and slips in to where I am.

"It's like taking out the egg stuff and leaving the shell," she says. "Teacher showed us last year. It was messy."

I give her the snippers. We saw and snip till we end up with a little cave room. Then we find stones for seats and move them in. There's just enough room for us both, our knees nearly touching. The sun fights its way through the leaves, forming yellow polka dots on our skin and clothes. The dots seem to dance over us, and I think about swimming underwater at the pool with my eyes open.

"Feels like a nest," Cassie says.

"Hey, it does," I say. "That's what we'll call it. Dragon's Nest."

"Do dragons have nests?"

"I don't know. They might. I'll ask Luke. But it's a good name, don't you think?"

She nods.

"We'll need to store some food," I say.

"Licorice. And mashed potatoes. They're my favorite."

"Licorice is okay. And maybe those beef jerkies Dad brings home. We can't have mashed potatoes, 'cause it'll go rotten. We need wrapped stuff . . . like candy bars."

"Kit Kats!" Cassie says.

"Well, save your money then. But the important thing is that now you have a place to go in case you get scared. And me too. And if something happens, and we can't find each other, we'll know where the other person is."

"Won't Dad be mad if he finds out?"

"He's not *finding* out!" I say. "Unless you tell. . . . Now go back outside and we'll test it."

When she's out, I tell her to walk all the way to the shed.

"You there?"

"Yeah."

"Now walk back like you're looking for something you left in the yard. Or pretend you're Dad checking to see if the grass needs mowing."

I wait.

"Can you see me?"

"No! I mean, I know where you are 'cause of the stick pile. But you're right . . . there's too many leaves." Her voice grows louder. "If I get right up close to the hedge with my face—like this—then I can see pieces of your shirt."

"Told ya," I say as I come out. "I couldn't see you either, 'cept right at the end. Now we gotta ditch the evidence."

I get a trash bag from the shed. We put in all the branches and sticks and drag the bag around to Mrs. Pittmon's. There's already a bunch of bags in the corner of the yard, so I'm sure she won't mind.

We go back to Dragon's Nest and toss a few sticks we missed into the hedge. "Now we have to cross our hearts," I say. "And promise not to tell and never to let anyone see us going in or coming out."

We sign crosses. I make sure to put the saw and snippers back exactly like they were. When we go inside for a drink, Mom's cleaning out the kitchen cabinet drawers. She's got silverware and junk piled all over. "I figured the next time I cleaned these drawers we'd be moving to a house with a *real* kitchen," she says. "You guys want a sandwich for lunch?"

"Mashed potatoes!" Cassie says.

"Not for *lunch*," Mom says. She grabs the peanut butter and jam from the fridge. "What've you been up to all this time, anyway?"

I give Cassie a look. "Just playing," I say.

That night, Cassie's putting down paper towels for napkins and I'm counting out forks and spoons when Dad comes in the back door. He winks at me, one hand behind his back, then clears his throat to get Mom to turn his way. "Is this the residence of Roxanne Wasniewski?" he says, bowing at the waist.

Mom squints, grins. "You look like the cat who swallowed the canary. What's eating you?"

It's the most they've said to each other in two days.

"Nothing's eating me," Dad says. "Only that I

been thinking, and I don't see why we need to get all riled up over a few silly bills and a couple of lottery tickets."

His tongue darts out to wet his lips.

"And I want you all to know that I'm plannin' to find a different job for the winter. A better one. This year, come the holidays, it'll be better."

"No more *shitty* jobs," Cassie says, her hand snapping up too late to cover her mouth.

Dad swallows a laugh. I have to press my lips together. Mom shakes her head. "Now, Cassie, that's not a nice word to use. You know that." She looks at Dad. "Even if you've heard *other people* say it, it's a bad word."

"It was in the front of my brain," Cassie says. "It just spilled out."

Mom's shoulders drop and a smile sneaks over her face. That's when Dad brings his hand from behind his back and offers a skinny bouquet of flowers with the Safeway sticker still on the green plastic wrapping.

Mom brings the bouquet up to her nose. "Well," she says, her eyes all shiny. "Well."

Cassie gives a tug on my shirt. I meet her smile with a confident nod, like I knew all along that Dad and Mom would make up.

After supper the four of us play Monopoly. We squeeze around the board, which is on the floor between the TV and the sofa. It's the first game we've played together in a long time. Cassie and I are a team. Mom's money pile is the biggest. "You should be in real estate," Dad tells her.

Cassie's in charge of the Cheetos. She counts out four whenever anyone passes GO.

"Jake, why don't you and Cassie get us some pop," Mom says after a while.

"You have to wait," Cassie says. "No cheating."

I go to the fridge while Cassie gets the glasses. There's beer by the cola, two cans. "Dad, did you want something?"

"I'll take a pop," he says right away.

I reach for the bottle of cola, my webbed toes happy-tapping the floor.

"You only got two glasses," I tell Cassie.

"I know," she says with a giggle. She's down on her knees reaching into one of the bottom cupboards.

"What're you doin'?"

"I saw these yesterday when I was helping Mom put away the pots." She gets up and shows me two plastic cups.

"Those?" I say. "Those are ancient. Those are sippy cups. From when we were little."

"I know," she says, her voice falling to a whisper. "Let's put Mom and Dad's pop in them."

I'm like one of those bobblehead dolls. This is one of Cassie's best ideas ever.

We each take a sippy cup to the living room. "Here, Dad," Cassie says. I hand mine to Mom.

"What's this?" Mom says. "Oh, my *God,* where'd you find those?"

"You *have* to use them," Cassie says sternly. "So

you don't spill. You know how messy you two can be."

"Oh, well," Dad says, playing along. "If we have to."

He clicks his red plastic cup to Mom's blue one. Then they sip-suck until they get some pop. When they're done, they smack their lips. Dad pulls in his shoulders to make himself small.

"Goo-Goo," he tells Mom.

"Gaa-Gaa," Mom says back.

It's impossible not to laugh.

"Now you know what's it like to be a kid," Cassie says.

"I'm pretty sure I *was* a kid once," Mom says. "I might even have the photos to prove it."

"Just as long as you don't find any diapers around here," Dad tells Cassie. "That's one experience Mom and I don't need to relive."

Picturing Mom and Dad in diapers is too much for Cassie. She spins to the floor, holding her stomach.

I get the other two pops from the kitchen. We

just start playing again when the phone rings. I run to answer it. It's Luke.

"Don't eat bananas," he says.

"What?"

"I just found out. Mosquitoes are attracted to people who eat bananas. I think that's why I get bit so much."

"You're crazy," I say.

"And flamingos can only eat with their heads upside down. I know, I can't believe it either. I also can't believe school's starting in three days. I'm not ready. Are you?"

"I wish the pool wasn't closing," I say.

"Me too. So are you going to try it?"

"Try what?"

"See what it's like to be a flamingo."

I picture myself standing on my head, eating a banana and getting buzzed by mosquitoes. "I don't think so."

"Well, I am. I'll let you know."

"Luke, wait . . . do dragons have nests?"

"The flying ones do. Why?"

"Just wondered. Thanks. See ya."

When I get back to the game Dad's handing over another stack of money to Mom.

"You're rich, Mommy," Cassie says.

Mom counts the new bills and puts them in her bank. She can't stop smiling. "I feel lucky," she says.

I take the dice and let Cassie blow Cheetos breath over them. Then I shake them hard in my hands, feeling lucky too.

Chapter Six

ACCORDING TO LUKE, the smallest bat in the world is the bumblebee bat. "It's like holding a dime in your hand. If you closed your eyes, you wouldn't even know it's there." I asked him if it still looks like a bat—big ears and all—and he said, "Duh." So now whenever I think of the bumblebee bat, I think of a dime with ears. If I had a bumblebee bat in my hand, I'd open my fingers and show it to people. They'd be amazed.

I came to like bats after Dad took me to Paul's for a haircut in June. I was still in fourth grade. Dad looked me over one Saturday and said, "You look like a damn sheepdog. Let's go see Paul."

Paul the Barber is a big man with silver hair. He wears a white coat to protect himself from flying hair. There's always an old dead cigar in the ashtray on his countertop. A sign on the wall says NO SMOK-ING, but I don't think Paul pays any attention to it when the shop is empty.

"Hey, pardner," Paul said when me and Dad walked in. I sniffed in the familiar smells of old cigar and hair goop, and looked at the jar of Tootsie Roll Pops on the counter.

"Pick out two for you and two for your sister," Paul said with a smile. "I'll be with you in a minute."

I'm pretty sure Paul was a cowboy before he became a barber because there's an old harness and a saddle on the wall. And pictures of him with horses. He looks a lot younger in the pictures. And different too, without his big belly. He uses his belly now to spin the barber chair where he wants. Like having another hand.

"Cut it off!" Dad said when I climbed into the chair. "All of it. Too hot for a boy to be running around with a mop on his head."

"I don't want to be bald," I said.

Paul cinched the apron around my neck. "You won't be bald, just lighter."

He pumped the chair's foot lever, and up I rose, like someone important, facing the lights and mirrors. I pictured a TV reporter sticking a microphone in front of my face: *Any last words?*

I looked into the mirror at the thick hair that flopped onto my forehead and over my ears. I tried to smile for the cameras, but the face in the glass looked scared. *Good-bye hair,* I told the microphone.

Paul started up the clippers with its low vibrating sound. He began at the back of my head on one side, and made a swipe all the way over the top to my forehead. He made another pass, then another. Before I knew it, one side had hair, and the other, no hair.

"What say . . . should we leave it like this?" Paul

asked, holding the clippers away from me and looking into the glass.

I thought of Mrs. Sinclair and the kids at school and how surprised everyone would be if I walked in Monday morning with a Mohawk. "I don't think so."

"You're probably right," Paul said. He started making swipes again. Back to front. Mowing my head. Gobs of hair falling onto my apron.

"There," he said finally. "Clean as a whistle."

I rubbed my fingers through the bristly hairs. It felt funny, like rubbing Dad's old shoe brush, the one he uses on his good black shoes. I kind of liked the feel.

Paul brushed away some stray hairs that stuck to my ears and neck. He took off the apron and shook all my old hair onto the floor.

"There you go, son," he said. "Make your dad proud. You look like a young soldier."

Did I look like a soldier? Like an army man? Dad had been a soldier for a while. He says the army made a man of him. I wanted to be a man too. I stood a little straighter when I got out of the chair.

Dad also got his hair cut. Just as short as mine, which made me feel like we were army men together. I brushed my palm back and forth over my new head all the way home.

When I got to school on Monday, everyone noticed my hair.

"You got scalped, Jake!"

"What happened?"

"You're bare naked!"

Some of the kids wanted to touch my head, just to see what it felt like. Mrs. Sinclair said I was going to be the coolest person in the room come afternoon when the sun beat against the blinds. "You look very nice," she said.

I felt pretty nice too, until later when Mrs. Sinclair read the class *Stellaluna,* a book about a bat. After the story, we talked about bats. Most kids had never seen a bat except on TV. One girl tried to say she'd been attacked by one, but everyone knew she was lying.

Mrs. Sinclair said bats don't usually attack people. They send out high-pitched sounds and use the returning echoes to figure out what's around them and where things are. The echoes let them know when they need to turn away from a tree or where a tasty moth is.

"Like radar?"

"Something like that," Mrs. Sinclair said.

"Like sonar . . . like in submarines."

"Yes," she said. "That's why their ears are so big, so they can catch the sound waves."

"Like Jake's ears?" someone said.

Everybody laughed and spun around to look at me.

"No," the teacher said. "Jake has people ears."

"But they stick out like a bat's."

"You got sonar, Jake?"

"Hey, we could call you Batman!"

"Maybe Jake doesn't want a nickname," Mrs. Sinclair said. "Do you, Jake?"

"NO!" I said.

I thought about my ears all the way home. They actually felt big now. Way big. I was sure I could feel them flap a little as I walked. By the time I got home my stomach was all twisted with worry.

"Mom, I've got humongous ears, don't I?"

"What? What's wrong with your ears?"

"They're huge. That's what the kids at school say. They say I look like a bat."

"Your ears are fine," she said. "Most kids have big ears. Then their faces and heads grow into them. Your ears are fine. They're beautifully shaped."

"You sure?"

I flicked the tops of both ears back and forth and studied them in the mirror. They looked pretty big.

"They stick out," I said.

"They're supposed to stick out. That's why they're ears."

"How come they never stuck out before?"

"Because you had a mop of hair covering your face. Nothing could stick out."

"Stand proud," Dad said when I told him what the kids were saying. "Be a man."

The thing is, though, after the bat-ear thing at school I got really interested in bats. I checked out all the books on bats from the school library. I couldn't read most of the words, but the pictures were cool. Once I told Luke about bats, he started to like them too. He added bats to his list of Amazing Things to Know. What I like best about bats is that they're different. People think they're weird. But they're not. They're just another kind of animal . . . with big ears.

When Mom found out I liked bats, her nose crinkled. "They're disgusting," she said. "Like rats with wings."

"No," I said. I told her how they hang upside down so they can get a running start at flying . . . how they stay together in colonies and help one another . . . how the parents love the pups, which is what the babies are called.

She still made a face. But for my birthday in July

she got me a poster of a flying fox—the largest bat there is. The poster's taped to the wall near my bed. The bat's face looks more like a dog's than a fox's . . . like a wiener dog or Chihuahua. It's hanging upside down from a branch, rubbery wings folded cozy over its body, all tucked in and ready to sleep.

Sometimes at night when Mom and Dad are arguing and Cassie doesn't wake up for a story, I look hard at the poster. I look and look, thinking if I look hard enough something good might happen. Like I might change right there, sprout real bat ears and see-through leather wings and go flying into the night, soaring across Fremont Street to Luke's house where I'll hover outside his bedroom window, making clicking noises through the screen till he wakes up. He'll rub his eyes . . . to make sure what he's seeing's for real.

JAKE?

'Course it's me. You know any other bats that hang out at your bedroom window?

Are they fighting again?

I won't even have to think about such things. I'll just fly off. Out into the middle of a summer night. Where it's cool. No sweaty sheets. Nothing being knocked over or thrown against the wall. No swear words. Just me and the cricket choir *chir-chirring*.

Sometimes I make it so Luke can become a bat too, and join me. But mostly it's just me, soaring over the rooftops, my moon shadow racing the cars in the lighted streets below.

By the time I fly back to our house, the yelling has stopped. I can hear Dad snoring. I slip back through the window, bringing in some cool night for Cassie, her breathing clearing as she rolls over onto her back and sighs, pulling Thumper closer.

Chapter Seven

CASSIE'S BEEN STRAPPED into her Barbie backpack since she got dressed. "Come on, Jake, we'll be late!"

I'm looking through the basket of clean laundry, trying to find a pair of socks without holes. Last year on the first day Mrs. Sinclair took us to the gym to play a game called Crab Soccer. The ball was so big it took three kids to roll it out of the storage room. We had to take off our shoes and crab walk on our hands and feet, keeping our butts off the floor. It was fun, except my toes were sticking out of my socks like they were saying hi to everyone.

Ducking into the bathroom, I check to make sure I don't have any milk or gunk on my face. I rub what's left of my hair and flick my fresh bat ears for good luck. Yesterday Dad took me to Paul's for a back-to-school haircut. He said it was up to me, if I wanted it short again. "Take it all off," I told Paul. He did.

"Are you sure you don't want me to walk you?" Mom says.

I remind her that I'm a fifth grader now.

"And I'm a second grader!" Cassie says.

Cassie wants to run the six blocks to school, but I tell her to take it easy. I'm a little worried about seeing everyone after so long. A lot can happen over the summer. You never know if your buddy in June still wants to be friends in September.

Luke says he's always terrified on the first day of school. *Terrified.* That's the word he uses. He has nightmares about it. Last week he dreamed the teacher ground up this kid she didn't like and made chicken nuggets out of his parts. Luke warned everyone not to eat the nuggets, but they all thought he was crazy.

I wish Luke didn't go to St. Joe's. It'd be great to be in the same class with him.

School is mobbed when we get there. Parents and kids crowd the office window, checking the class lists. Me and Cassie already know our rooms and teachers. Mom gave in to Cassie's bugging and called the school office last week, saying she'd be out of town the first day of school and could she please know her kids' classes.

I make sure Cassie finds one of her friends, then head for the fifth-grade wing.

"Hey!" Jeremy Sorrell says. He and David Mackie have a new playground ball with David's name on it and are taking turns slamming it against the brick.

"Hey," I say back.

They're both wearing new basketball shoes, white and black and green with silver emblems. Their jeans and shirts are new too. I look down at my sneakers. Mom says already-worn-in shoes are better for your feet than new ones. If my feet could talk, they'd say "Yeah, right."

Andy Tolbert drops his pack in front of Room 11. "RIBBET!" he yells really loud. "Hey, Ribbet. . . . We're in the same class again!"

I want to tell him to lay off calling me Ribbet this year . . . tell him he's a big-mouthed jerk. But with guys like Andy, if you say you don't want them to do something they'll just do it worse.

When the bell rings we file inside. The desk with my name is in the back, in a group of six, with Andy, Molly, Devon, Joanna, and a new girl named Michelle.

The teacher, Mr. Wyatt, spends all morning talking about how great a year we're going to have if we all follow the rules. Problem is, there are about a hundred rules. We get to the cafeteria for lunch just as the little kids are being excused for recess. Cassie runs over to my table before she goes out to the playground, pulling another girl with her. "This is my brother," she says, like she's giving a tour of the Statue of Liberty or something.

"Hi," the girl says, then giggles. That starts Cassie giggling. With their front teeth missing, they look like two happy jack-o'-lanterns.

Mr. Wyatt is new to the school. He must think we're all smart. After lunch he wants everyone to write about themselves. "At least a page," he says, "but you'll probably end up writing much more than that."

I hear a few gulps, including mine.

"I'll write a lot more," Andy says. "We went to Yellowstone. A million things happened."

"I love to write," Michelle says. "Don't you?"

She's looking at me, looking across our two desks. She asked me a question and now she's waiting for an answer. I shrug. Like I don't understand. Like I can't speak the language. Maybe she'll think I'm one of the Spanish- or Russian-speaking kids.

My stomach is one big knot as I get out a sheet of

paper. It takes me a long time to get the heading right, copying from the sample on the overhead.

Mr. Wyatt is walking around the room, commenting on everyone's work. I feel him stop behind me. He'll probably tell me I'm slow as molasses . . . slow as a tortoise . . . a snail. I've heard them all before.

He's still standing there, not saying anything as I move the pencil. I lift my finger from the pencil and shake my hand like it hurts. Maybe he'll think I've got a sprain or a broken finger. He just waits. I start from where I left off. *My name is Jake and I whont to be a doktir or a sinetist but I'm prolly not smar—*

"You have nice handwriting, Jake."

The suddenness of his voice makes me jump. I wait for the rest: *Maybe you could speed it up a bit. Put it in second gear.* But it doesn't come. He moves on toward the front of the room and asks for everyone's attention.

"Some people are better at drawing than writing," he says. "If you want, instead of writing everything out, you can draw little snapshots of who you are. Snapshots of what's important to you . . . your family, pets, hopes. Stuff like that."

I look at Desiree across the way. She smiles, like she's as happy as I am to hear that we can draw instead of write. Austin too. All of us in the LEP class. It's like we all give a big sigh of relief, then start in on our drawings.

I fold my paper into fourths. On one side I draw me, Cassie, Mom, and Dad. On the other side I draw a flying fox, Nina and Otto on their cushions, Mrs. Pittmon's wheelchair, and the Vista Park Pool. Michelle says I'm a good drawer. When she's done writing, she draws a dog in the margin of her paper. "I'm not very good," she says.

After that, Mr. Wyatt teaches us a game called Categories. Each group is a team. We have to name things that begin with certain letters. When we get to naming a mammal that starts with B, I tell Molly to write down *bat.*

"You sure?" Andy says.

"Positive," I say.

Each group gets a point only if no other group thought of the same answer. Two groups say *buffalo,* and two say *bear.* We're the only ones with *bat.*

"*Bat* gets a point," Mr. Wyatt says.

"Way to go, Jake!"

"How'd you know a bat is a mammal?" Mr. Wyatt asks me.

I want to say because I'm smart. Or that my friend Luke is smart and we've talked about it. Or that a guy with ears like mine has to know about his fellow bats.

"I dunno," I say.

The best thing about the first day is that the LEP kids get to go to Mrs. Maw's for a Welcome Back party.

"Jake," Mrs. Maw says when she sees me. "You look great! Did you have a nice summer?" She winks and lowers her voice. "Don't forget . . . this is your year."

I nod, my face heating up.

Tyler, a college student and Mrs. Maw's new assistant, is the tallest teacher I've ever seen. He gives me a thumbs-up and tells me to help myself to the juice and cookies.

I look around the room. Billy, Damian, Cerise, and a few others from last year are also here. Purple and yellow balloons hang from the ceiling. There are fresh posters on the wall. Everything looks shiny new.

Mrs. Maw calls us over to the circular table and tells us about the school's new reading program. "Your teachers will be telling the rest of your classes about it sometime soon, but I wanted my kids to have a sneak preview."

She points to a shelf filled with books. The spine of each book has a colored circle taped to it. Some are green, some pink, some blue, and some orange.

"The program is called Everyone Reads. Each book in the school with a colored dot will be an E-R book. That means there's a computer test you can take whenever you finish a story. The tests show if you understand what you've read."

"What'll we get if we pass the test?"

"You'll probably find you're becoming a better reader," Tyler the Tall says.

"Plus, you earn points," Mrs. Maw says. "When you reach a certain number of points you'll earn special privileges. We might even celebrate from time to time as we progress—parties and that kind of thing. Of course, I understand that fifth graders are too old for parties."

"WHAT?"

"Not fair! No way can fourth graders get parties and we can't."

Mrs. Maw shrugs. "Well, then, parties it'll be, as long as you read more than you've ever read before."

That night at supper Cassie says her teacher, Miss Hannah, is the best teacher in the world because she lets them paint and doesn't care if they make a mess.

"She says we're gonna put on lots of puppet shows. And Missy, Christopher and I are best friends again. Julie Langer says all girls with Barbie backpacks have to stay together and be best friends all year no matter if you get sick of each other or not."

Mom and Dad smile. I roll my eyes.

"We got homework too," Cassie adds. "On the first day!"

"How 'bout you, Jake?" Mom says. "Did it go all right for you?"

"Mr. Wyatt seems okay," I say.

"Are you still going to be with Mrs. Maw for reading?"

I nod. "I already checked out four books. Mrs. Maw wants us to get a jump on the rest of the school. There's a new reading program this year."

"Good," Mom says. "I'm glad you'll be with Mrs. Maw again. I like her."

Dad leans back in his chair. "Maybe you can work your way out of that class this year."

"Maybe," I say.

"Do they still call it Bonehead Reading? That's what we called it when I was in school."

I feel a sudden burning behind my eyes.

"Rob . . . please," Mom says.

"Take it easy," Dad says. "I didn't mean it the way it came out. It's a *joke!*"

I leave the table without finishing my food. Cassie leaves too, in a hurry to get to her homework. She gets jealous when she sees the books I checked out from Mrs. Maw's. "How come you get library books on the first day?"

Her face switches from *no fair* to *hope*. "Will you share, Jake? Will you read them to me too?"

"I'll think about it," I say.

I take the four books outside and sit against the back of the garage in the after-supper sun. I need to practice so I don't make too many mistakes when I read the stories to Cassie. It's hard to concentrate, though. I keep thinking about what Dad said. The burning feeling builds up again and a few tears leak out, but I wipe them away. In my mind I see a dog bone with my head on it. *Bonehead Jake.*

"It's a *joke!*" I tell the yard and the hedge and the whole stupid sky.

"HA, HA," I say. "HA, HA, HA."

Chapter Eight

*M*OM WANTS TO HAVE a yard sale. "While the weather's still decent," she says. She thinks people will buy our old stuff. They'd have to be pretty hard up if you ask me, but she doesn't. She and Cassie are going through the closets as Dad and I finish our breakfasts.

"I hate yard sales," Dad says. "You put all your stuff out there to be pawed over by complete strangers."

"Then keep all your precious *stuff!*" Mom calls from the living room. "You should be glad I'm trying to bring in some extra money."

Dad goes back to reading the sports section. He picked up the paper when he went out for cigarettes. It's unusual for him to have a Saturday off work, and I can tell he's glad. He even sat and watched cartoons with me and Cassie before breakfast, laughing at all the right spots.

I finish my cereal and put the bowl in the sink, thinking I'll go see Mrs. Pittmon.

"Jake," Dad says, waving me back to the table. "I've been thinking about that special class you're in. I don't get it. You've always got your head in a book around here. How can that teacher at school say you can't read?"

"I can read," I say. "Just not so good."

"Bet you can read better than you think," he says, sliding the newspaper over to me and pointing to an article. "Here, give this a try."

The story is about the Mariners baseball team. The print looks small, the words big. "I don't feel like reading now," I say.

"Just a little," he says. "Go ahead."

I focus on the words. "Last year," I begin. "Last year

the team re . . . keev-ed . . . two minner lag-u-ee player—"

"*Re-keeved?*" Dad says. "Come on, now. You ever heard of a word *re-keeved?*" His finger taps beneath the word.

I try to think if I heard it.

"Have you?"

"Prob'ly not," I say.

"No . . . 'course not. No such word as *re-keeved.* Right?"

"Right."

"I'm just trying to help," he says. "You know that, right?"

I nod. "I guess I don't feel much like reading right now."

"Sorry . . . but this is when I got some time. You want to get better at reading, dontcha?"

I nod.

"Then you have to practice. No pain, no gain. . . . Jake, you can look at me when I'm talking to you."

I look, but not at his eyes. I'm afraid of what I

might see there. Disgust. Disgust at having a kid who can't read worth beans. I look at the hairs poking out his nostrils instead, at the stubble of whiskers over his lip.

"Re-*ceived*," he says finally. "The team *received* two . . ." He points to the next word and spells it. "M-i-n-o-r. Either *meener* or *miner*, right?"

I'm staring at the paper. At his finger. There's a little black blister near the nail.

"You got a blister."

"Never mind my blister. Meener or miner, right?"

"Right."

"Well . . . which makes sense?"

". . . Received two minor lee—" I say.

"*League* is hard," he says. "I'll grant you that. . . . Keep going."

"Dad, I . . ."

He takes my finger and puts it on the paper, below the line he wants me to read. I feel my throat close up and the burning start in the back of my eyes. I press down hard with the tip of my finger.

The words and letters get blurry. I press so hard, the paper gives way, my finger pushing through and up underneath the other side.

I hear the slap, then feel it, my cheek suddenly on fire.

"You did that on purpose!"

I take off. For the laundry room and the back door.

"Come back here!"

I keep running. Behind the garage. To the back of the yard . . . the hedge . . . to Dragon's Nest, where I slip through the green into cool darkness, the tight net of branches and leaves keeping the light out. I sit with my knees up, out of breath, thoughts flying through my head. How I hate our house. Hate school. Hate holey socks. Hate cheap sneakers that look good at the store but fall apart the next week. Hate bills and houses with tiny bedrooms you have to share with your baby sister and lottery tickets that never win nothing.

I squeeze to keep the tears from spilling out, but I

can't. They burst right through. No stopping them or the spinning, sick feeling in my stomach.

"Jake?"

My ears prick to full alert. A whisper. From Mrs. Pittmon's side of the hedge.

"Cassie?"

"Yeah, it's me."

I suck up nose goop, swallow it. "Cassie, go away."

Twigs catch and snap as she squeezes through the green wall. Breathing hard, she wiggles herself onto her stone, a long red scratch curving down one arm.

"I came around Mrs. P.'s side," she says. "It's safer."

Now that I can think again, I know what a good idea it is, coming into Dragon's Nest from Mrs. P.'s side. Much less likely to be seen. I should have thought of it.

She studies my face. "I can see Daddy's fingers," she says.

I touch the place gently. The burning is like a light blinking on and off. "Doesn't hurt that bad," I say.

"It was loud," she says. "The slap. Mommy and I heard it all the way in our room. We ran to see what happened. Mommy called Daddy a bully. She said she hated living like this . . . that the family was falling apart. I don't like Daddy anymore."

"Yes, you do," I say. But I'm thinking more about what *I* did. Maybe it wasn't all Dad's fault. Maybe he was right. Maybe I *did* do it on purpose . . . *tried* to poke my finger through . . . *wanted* to tear the stupid newspaper.

"JAKE!"

Dad's voice. We freeze.

"Jake, I'm sorry. . . . Come on back now."

I put a finger up to my lips.

"Come on, son, I said I was sorry."

Cassie's teeth are pressed into her bottom lip. I feel my ears pounding in time with my heart. But his voice hasn't gotten closer. He must be at the back door, on the little patio. Looking. Listening. Waiting for me to come running.

Another few seconds and the door to the house

slams shut. Cassie and I start breathing again. I take a Kit Kat from the Star Wars plastic pencil box that holds our provisions. "Here," I say, splitting the candy in half. "Eat."

She takes a bite and chews. "It works," she says. "Dragon's Nest works."

Chocolate floods my mouth. "I shouldn't have gotten mad," I say after a while. "Shouldn't have done what I did. We don't want to be a falling-apart family, do we?"

She shakes her head, the corners of her mouth pooled with chocolate.

"Then we can't make Dad mad."

Chapter Nine

On Monday Mr. Wyatt says each group needs to pick a name. Then we can make a poster and hang it from the ceiling above our desks. "We could make it a theme—like birds of prey, or sports, or something goofy, like appliances. Or do you want it totally open to whatever?"

"We'll be the toasters," someone says.

"The Mariners."

"Falcons."

"The Corvettes!" Andy says to our group. "We can be the Corvettes. They're the best!"

"We'd have to draw one. Cars are hard."

"I can draw one. I've got a poster at home."

Mr. Wyatt suggests food for a theme.

"The banana splits."

"The Jolly Ranchers."

"That's candy. He said *food*."

"I don't want to be a broccoli!"

Mr. Wyatt gives up. "Okay, no theme. Just pick something and have your posters done by Friday."

"We could be bats," I say.

"Bats are ugly," Michelle says. "They're scary-looking. And they drink blood."

"Just the vampire bats drink blood," I say. "All the other kinds eat insects or fruit or fish."

"Fish!" Molly says. "Bats don't eat fish."

"Yes, they do . . . some of 'em."

"They'd be easy to draw," Joanna says.

"We could have them hanging from the poster, hanging on string like they're flying," Devon says.

Andy holds out for Corvettes.

We take a vote. Me and Joanna and Devon go

for bats. Andy and Molly and Michelle go for Corvettes.

"Now what?" Andy says.

"Have you decided?" Mr. Wyatt says to the class.

Everyone else has. There are the Wizards, the Microwaves, the Banana Splits, the Cheetahs. . . .

"Let's be something weird," Devon says.

I try to think of something weird. All I can think of are feet. Because this morning Dad had to put a wrap on his ankle before he went to work. He stepped wrong climbing down a ladder. The skin was black and blue. Dad put his foot on a kitchen chair while he pulled on the skin-colored wrap.

"Your toes have hair, Daddy," Cassie said.

"What, you don't like my toes?" Dad said, pretending to be hurt.

"Feet are weird," Cassie announced, like she'd made an important scientific discovery.

"FEET ARE WEIRD," I suddenly blurt out, surprised to have said it out loud.

Everyone looks at me like I'm an alien.

I shrug. "You know, feet."

"Feet stink," Andy says. Then his face lights up. "Hey . . . the Stinky Feet!"

Michelle giggles. Devon's head bobs up and down. "We could hang up old socks."

"Not stinky ones," Joanna says. "We have to sit under them, you know."

They look at me. I guess we're voting.

"I like stinky feet," I say. "I mean—"

We all burst out laughing.

After school I run over to see Mrs. Pittmon. Mom said we're having a sale with or without Dad, and that I should ask Mrs. P. if she has anything she wants to sell.

"A yard sale, you say?"

Clippers in one hand, watering can in the other, Mrs. Pittmon fusses with one of the plants lined up in clay pots around the little back patio of her house. She uses her elbows to wheel her chair.

"Cassie has different-colored stickers for price tags, so we know who gets the money. She's putting yellow stickers on Mom's stuff, and green on mine and hers—we're going in together. I think she has orange left. Your stuff could be orange."

Mrs. P. looks out into the tiny yard where a squirrel stands like a statue beside the fence. Otto appears suddenly from the side of the house and gets down in his stalking pose, but the squirrel flits off before any hunt can begin.

"I've got a bunch of new plant starts," she says. "Angel wings and grape and holly. A ton of old pots too." She points the clippers at me. "Do people still like houseplants, or are plants too low-tech for today's crowd?"

"Mom likes plants," I say. "If they don't die on her."

The sun has turned Mrs. P.'s glasses into mirrors. They look like racing goggles. She could be a racer . . . in one of those wheelchair races I've seen on TV. I picture me wheeling Mrs. P. up to the starting line, shouting out last-minute instructions: *Stay*

close to the leader till the last curve, then put your shoul-
ders into it and let 'er rip!

She plucks a ripe cherry tomato from one of the plants and tosses it to me. "There's some old blankets and bedclothes I won't be needing anymore. I been saving them for when the kids come to visit, but they don't come. Don't call, neither. Sweet, huh?"

I nod.

She reaches into the zippered pouch that hangs from one arm of her chair. I expect her to pull out the notepad she keeps there, but she lifts up a cell phone instead.

"My daughter gave it to me last Christmas. Know how many times we've talked since then?"

I shake my head.

She lifts up two fingers. "And both times it was for something she wanted me to do for her. Find this, send that." She plops the phone back into the pouch.

"Mom and Dad had a cell phone once," I say. "But it cost too much money."

"Not that expensive . . . if you never use it." She chuckles. "Oh, me—how silly is that?"

"Pretty silly," I say.

We go inside, and I clean out the cats' bowls and use a cup to pick the hard stuff from the litter box.

At the sound of the can opener, Otto comes barging through the cat door and Nina zips in from The Bead Room. I portion out half a can of soft food to each.

"How's school?" Mrs. P. asks when I'm cleaning up.

I shrug. "Okay."

"I'll bet you're a good student."

I could say whatever I want and Mrs. P. would never know the truth. Could say I get all A's. But I don't. "I'm not a real great reader," I mumble.

"Neither was I . . . when I was your age," she answers.

"You weren't?"

"Had a heck of a time keeping the letters and

words from getting all mixed up. I had to train myself to stop the letters from moving around. I'd say 'dog' instead of 'god' and 'Sally' instead of 'silly.'"

"Mrs. Maw says I need to concentrate. She says I have to have it totally quiet and really concentrate because I get distracted by things."

"What things are those?"

I picture the kids at school sighing and moving in their seats whenever it's my turn to read.

"Sounds mostly. Like people whispering or moving things." I think of other sounds, loud ones—shouting and name-calling. But I keep those to myself.

Mrs. P. points to Nina and Otto, who are already lying out on the kitchen floor after eating. "Too bad we can't be like cats," she says. "Look at those two. . . . A bomb could go off and they'd only lift their heads to yawn before getting back down to their business."

"It'd take more than a bomb to distract them from their food," I say.

"Ain't that the truth. Well, if you ever need a quiet place to read, you're welcome to come here. It's quiet as death in this house most of the time. You could come over after school. . . . That's when the cats and I take our afternoon naps. 'Course if you wanted to read to me, that'd be even better. I'd give up any nap for a good story."

"I don't think so," I say. "I'm a real slow reader. . . . You'd forget what's happening in the story. That's what happens to me. You'd get bored."

"Ha!" she says. "That'd work out fine too. You could put me to sleep. I'd get my nap and you'd get your practice. Well, you think about it. When's the yard sale?"

"Not this Saturday, but the next one," I say.

"Hmmm, that's close to two weeks." She gives a pretend *oof* as Nina jumps up onto her lap, and helps the cat into a sit with the palm of her hand. The room becomes a giant purr.

"That gives you and Otto two weeks to shape

up," she tells Nina. "Otherwise it's an orange sticker for both of you and a couple of bucks in my pocket."

I smile when I think of Nina purring at the yard sale, an orange sticker on her forehead.

Chapter Ten

It RAINS ALL DAY Tuesday. Cassie and I get drenched on the way home from school. It's like someone told God the Earth is on fire and he turned on the sky-hose to drown it out. After the first block, we don't even try to stay dry. We get goofy instead, stomping through puddles and lifting our faces to the pouring rain, mouths open for a drink. We end up soaked to the skin by the time we reach the house. "We're home!" Cassie calls, throwing open the front door.

We drop our backpacks and peel off our jackets.

Mom looks through to the living room from the kitchen table. "Oh my God! What'd you do, swim home? Jake, run and get some towels."

My shoes make squishy sounds across the floor to the bathroom. Cassie takes off her sneakers, and I throw a towel across the room at her. "It was fun, Mom," she says, her wet toes printing through her socks onto the floor.

"Don't be dripping on my stuff," Mom says. "All I need is to have my application tossed out because it's got wet spots on it."

My ears perk up. "But you have a job," I say, toweling under the neck of my shirt.

"This is for a real job. A receptionist."

"A *what?*" Cassie says. She coughs once, and Mom's eyes go on alert. I wait for another cough too, thinking the rain or the laughing might have triggered her. But none comes.

"Go put some dry socks on, young lady," Mom says. "In fact you should both change everything and throw those clothes in the dryer. Go on. Can't afford anybody getting sick. Last time Cassie had to go in, cost a whole month's rent."

We change on opposite sides of the room, Cassie in front of her chest of drawers, and me in front of the shelves that Dad put up for my stuff. Cassie wants to know what a receptionist does.

"They tell you how long you're gonna have to sit in the waiting room," I say. "Like at the doctor's. They have to answer the phone too."

Cassie's face is hidden under a fresh shirt. She grunts, her head suddenly popping through the hole. "Mom is good at answering phones," she says.

She finishes before me and darts out. In a second I hear the TV. "You left your wet stuff on the floor!" I yell to her. She doesn't answer. I scoop up both our piles of clothes for the dryer. Once, Luke asked me if it's sexy undressing in front of a girl, even if it's your sister.

"Whaddya mean?" I said.

"You know . . . like . . . you get a tingly all over."

"No," I said. "I don't get a tingly. Mostly I get mad

'cause Dad promised we were gonna move to a house with more bedrooms a million years ago." I didn't tell him Cassie and I used to take baths together when we were little. Mom plunking us both in the tub . . . Dad making funny faces in the mirror as he shaved . . . me and Cassie putting on bubble-beards.

"Anyway," I said, "we mostly have our underwear on when we change. And we can say *Turn* if we don't want the other to look. We're sorta like twins, like the stuck-together kind."

I carry the wet clothes out to the laundry room. It used to be the back porch until Dad got permission from the landlord to make a little room out of it. There's a green-colored washer and dryer against one wall. The other walls have shelves full of cleaning stuff and other junk.

Mom's still working on her papers at the table. I start up the dryer, then hurry to plop down on the sofa to watch cartoons. Cassie comes out of the bathroom and stops in the kitchen to pick up a half roll of Ritz crackers before taking up her side of the sofa.

"You gotta share," I say.

She shakes her head but reaches into the package and pulls out three crackers for me. "No more," she says.

After a while Mom pulls a cigarette out of the pack on the table and goes outside to smoke. I can hear the rain drumming on the garbage can's metal lid when she opens the back door.

We watch two whole shows and Mom is clearing her papers off the table when Dad pulls into the driveway. Cassie leans over the sofa and waves out the window at him, but he doesn't see her. Dad lifts an arm to his forehead, keeping his head down against the rain. He comes in through the laundry room, stamping the water off.

"You take off those boots," Mom says right away.

My eyes switch from the TV to the kitchen. Sometimes the kitchen is like a whole other TV.

Dad's baseball cap looks like it fell in a puddle.

The shoulders of his army jacket have turned dark. I wonder how he managed to get any painting done in the rain.

"Hi, Rob," he says, talking in a high voice, making fun, pretending to be Mom. *"How was your day, honey?"*

"Hi, Rob," Mom imitates, too much sweet in her voice. *"How was your day, honey?"*

"My day sucked!" Dad says, taking off his jacket and reaching for one of the hooks in the laundry room. "How 'bout yours?"

"Not so great," Mom says. "You know my boss, the one fresh out of college? . . . He cut my hours. Already! I just started. Ticked me off enough I went down to the employment office and got a referral for a receptionist job at the county offices over on Gartner Street."

She puts the folder with her papers on top of the refrigerator.

"What's for dinner?" Dad says.

I get that feeling again. Like my stomach is a wet

towel and someone's squeezing the water out of it. Why does Dad always have to ask what's for dinner when Mom hasn't started anything yet?

"Tacos," Mom says, taking a can of refrieds from the cupboard and slamming it on the counter. "Tacos, tacos, tacos."

I turn back to the TV, where a cartoon kid with thick glasses jet-packs across the screen. There's music. But my ears reach back toward the kitchen.

"I should be able to speak Spanish by now," Dad says.

"What's that supposed to mean?"

Dad doesn't answer. He sits down on a chair and unlaces his boots.

Cassie pulls the Budweiser throw from its place on the top of the sofa. Wraps it around her.

Dad won the throw at the Beaverton Fireman's Carnival last summer. He knocked over all three of the heavy bottles with a softball. No one ever wins that game, at least not that I've seen. But Dad did. He's got a strong arm for being skinny like he is. Dad wanted to get a Felix the Cat clock, the one with the tail that moves back and forth. But Mom talked him into the throw for when we watch TV and it's damp in the house.

Mom's back at the cupboard, pots and pans crashing. "I'd like to start stacking some of this stuff in the laundry room. If you'd get all that crap out of there."

The cartoons seem far away now. All I can do is watch the kitchen TV. Watch . . . and listen. Dad looks hard at the can of beans, at Mom spooning the beans into the pot on the stove. He peels off his socks, wincing when he does the left one, the ankle wrap still in place, then tosses his boots into the laundry room. They land with a bang against the screen door.

"Hi, kids," he says, stepping in to check the mail on the phone table.

"Hi, Dad," Cassie squeaks.

"Hi," I say.

"Good day at school?"

"We made leaf prints," Cassie says. "I made one for you, Daddy, but it's not done yet."

He looks at me.

"Okay," I say.

He gives a little smile. Maybe everything will be okay. Dad just came in mad 'cause he had to work in the rain. Maybe his boss said something that ticked him off. A lot of things happen. A lot of things give a person a bad mood.

Like at school today. During silent reading. Andy snickered through his nose and said loud enough for our whole group to hear: "Geez, Jake, I read that book in first grade." All at once the little book was on fire in my hands. Joanna and Devon moved their eyes across the title, trying not to laugh. *Nate the Great and the Missing Key.*

It's easy to get in a bad mood.

Dad goes into the bathroom. Cassie's fingers have loosened their grip on the throw. She hums the song she sang to me last night about going to some animal fair that Miss Nishitani taught her class in music.

The commercial on TV shows a dog drinking a glass of milk and a cow chewing on a bone. They're at a table together. There's a cat too, eating a piece of cheese . . . and a mouse with a fish on his plate. "See life from the other side," the announcer says, the picture switching to people laughing and dancing on a beach. A koala bear watches the people on the beach from the top of a tree. "See Australia," the voice says.

"EV-ERY GODDAMN TIME!"

The words explode from behind the bathroom door, causing Cassie and me to jump.

"MUST BE TOO MUCH TO ASK."

It's the toilet again. Has to be. Dad hates it when the toilet isn't flushed.

I look at Cassie. I can't remember if it was me.

No. Not me. I didn't go. I don't think—

We hear the flush handle slam down and the water whooshing. "JUST TOO MUCH TO ASK."

I want to tell Cassie to scoot to our room. I want to scoot too. But Dad is already there. In the doorway.

"Just once I'd like to come home, go to the bathroom, and not have to see a goddamn Lincoln Log lying in the toilet."

I hear the pot moving on the stove.

"Hon . . . come on," Mom says. "Just let it go."

My shoulders are so tight they feel like they might spring apart.

"It doesn't happen *ev'ry time,*" I say.

Dad glares at me, puzzled, like he's trying to figure out a hard math problem. I glare back, my heart racing, expecting him to lunge at the sofa with his palm out, set my face on fire. I don't even care if he does. It's not true, what he said. He's a liar.

Something shifts in Dad's eyes. A tiny smile pulls at the corners of his mouth. I have to look away, afraid of whatever's churning inside my stomach. "Not ev'ry time," I tell my feet, in case they haven't heard. "Doesn't happen ev'ry time."

"Rob . . . honey . . . come and help me cut up the stuff."

I look up and see Dad's jaw change from screw-tight to regular, his lips unclamping.

"You're right, son," he says. "Not every time. It isn't every time . . . is it, Cassie?"

Cassie's tiny voice is hard to hear through the throw. "No, Daddy."

He turns then, grabs a beer from the fridge, and joins Mom at the counter, putting his arm around her and giving her a light kiss on the cheek when she turns toward him.

"You kids wash up and set the table."

"Cassie and me are gonna eat in here," I say, my hands still trembling a little.

"Are you asking or telling?" Dad says.

"Let them eat where they want," Mom says. "Besides, I want to tell you about this job."

Dad doesn't say anything, just starts chopping up tomatoes on the cutting board. I'm hunched into the soft back of the sofa, a pillow squeezed against my chest to hold in my heart.

Liar. Bully.

I shut my eyes to stop the thoughts and see myself unfurling my wings right there in the center of the room. "Omigosh!" Mom says when she sees.

She flings open the kitchen window, and Dad jerks back with his jaw dropped as I fly through, out of the house and up into the air. From the top of the sky I can't even see our tiny refried-bean house. I swoop and dive and rise, the air tickling my fur leather wings whirring. No bad moods. No knotted shoulders. No unflushed toilets.

That night the Beastie-Beasts attack the fortress of the Bat King.

"All looks lost," I tell Cassie. "Then one of the bat men raises his wings in anger. The sun bounces off the silver of his wings straight into the eyes of the lead Beastie-Beast, who can't see to keep charging. The bats know they're on to something. They make their wings even shinier."

"How do they do that?" Cassie wants to know.

"They paint them . . . paint them with a color called Moon, so that their wings become like mirrors. Then when the Beastie-Beasts charge the castle again—"

"The bats fly up and blind them!"

"Right," I say. "And no one in the whole kingdom can believe how the bats turned back the charge of the Beastie-Beasts."

"Wow!" Cassie says.

"Yeah," I say.

"So are the Beastie-Beasts gone forever?"

"No. . . . But they know they can't push around the bats anymore. Not without a fight. Now go to sleep. Story's over."

"Jake?"

"What?"

"I'm sorry I forgot to flush."

"You can't forget, Cassie. You know it makes Dad crazy. You can't ever forget again. Hear?"

"I won't. I promise."

I make a promise too . . . to myself. . . . I promise that if I ever get to be a dad, I'll never yell at my kid for such a stupid thing.

Chapter Eleven

MR. WYATT FINISHES the math lesson early and says we can start on our homework. We're finding the areas of shapes.

Michelle sits directly across from me, so close we could touch each other's faces. She wants to know if I ever get cold. "Without much hair like that," she says. Her shoulders jump up like someone dropped an ice cube down her back.

She's got thick brown hair. Some days she makes it into a ponytail. Today it hangs plain to her shoulders. It shifts a little with the shiver, then settles back.

"No," I say. "I'm used to it."

"Not even in winter?"

I don't tell her I had long hair last winter. "Nope."

"Bet your ears get red, though."

She's not dissing me. Her look is more like a scientist's. Like she's trying to figure just how red and cold ears the size of mine could get when the temperature drops below freezing.

Andy looks up from his notebook. "I'm already on number eighteen. We gotta measure something and find the area." He snickers. "How 'bout your ears, Jake? Can we measure your ears?"

"Only if we can measure your butt," I say right back.

Michelle laughs.

"Ha-ha," Andy says, but he shuts up.

I tighten my grip on my nubby pencil, and draw the rectangle for problem number four. *Slow and steady wins the race.* That's what Mrs. Maw says when someone has a hard time reading out loud. *Slow and steady wins the race.* But it's not true. Michelle and

Andy are always done before me. If Mrs. Maw wasn't so nice I'd tell her that her *slow and steady* idea stinks.

At five to eleven Mr. Wyatt tells everyone to put away the math and get ready for reading. That's when I'm supposed to go with Desiree and Austin to Mrs. Maw's.

"Come on, Jake," Desiree says as she walks by our group. Like she has to make sure I get to Mrs. Maw's on time. Like the world will end if I don't make it there exactly at eleven.

"Go ahead," I say, pretending to be getting something from my desk.

She rolls her eyes, but leaves. I want to wait today because the class is reading a story about World War II. Yesterday Mrs. Maw was out sick, and the LEPs got to stay in the room for reading. We had work to do, but I mostly listened.

Dad said his Granddad Louie was in that war. He jumped out of airplanes. Dropped down behind enemy lines and almost got killed lots of times. But he didn't. That's why Dad is here and why me and Cassie are here too.

I lower my head so Mr. Wyatt doesn't notice me. The story's about the German Nazis. There's a girl and her family that the Nazis are after and these other people are trying to help the family get away to safety. All the good people have to be really watchful. Really careful. They use code words so the Nazis don't know that they're trying to get the Jewish family to another country.

Today the girl in the story—her name is Annemarie—hears cars driving up to the farmhouse where she's staying. It's the middle of the night. And she hears heavy boots clomping through the kitchen. The soldiers want to know why there are so many people in the house. And the girl's mother says that everyone is here to say good-bye to an old aunt who died. She points to the casket in the middle of the room. But, really, there's no dead aunt in the casket. Something else is inside. Something that will get everyone in big trouble if the Germans find out. It's spooky.

"Have you ever had the feeling of being closed in?" Mr. Wyatt asks the class. "Ever had to be super watchful, like the Johansens? Careful of what you did or said? On guard all the time? It must have been hard to live in fear like this every day, don't you think?"

Two kids raise their hands.

"Once I broke our neighbor's window playing baseball," Barry says. "The neighbor wasn't home, so I just pretended it wasn't me. But I was worried about the police coming over to get me."

Mr. Wyatt looks confused. "And?"

"The neighbor told my dad and he sat me down and made me admit it. I got grounded for lying. But I didn't really lie, did I? How can it be lying if you don't say anything?"

"Did you intend to hide the truth?" Mr. Wyatt says.

"Uh . . . I guess so."

Some kids laugh, and Barry smiles. "My baseball landed in a birthday cake the lady had made. There was still some blue frosting stuck in between the seams of the ball when I got it back. So I licked it clean."

"Gross."

"Yuck."

"Thank you for that," Mr. Wyatt says. He calls on Emma next, a new girl from South America, who tells how once her family was followed by policemen who didn't wear uniforms. "They always watch you . . . and make sure you don't break any rules."

"It's worse when you're waiting for something bad to happen," David says. "Like the soldiers in the story, when they came the first time. You knew they were gonna check all the rooms. You knew something bad was gonna happen."

"Yeah," Michelle says without raising her hand. "You have to wait and be all nervous. Like when my grandma was in the hospital and the doctor said she was going to die. And we were just waiting."

Just waiting. Like at home when there's been a

fight and Dad goes out. And me and Cassie know Dad will be coming back. But we don't know what he'll be like. If he'll still be mad. Or maybe be all calmed down, and just slip into bed.

My hand shoots up.

"Jake?"

He must mean me. I lock my eyes on to the yellow-papered bulletin board above his head.

"One night Dad came home with a kazoo and he was playing it really loud. Cassie was asleep but I was up lying in my bed and I heard the car come in the driveway and then the key in the lock and the door opening and the next thing I almost jumped outta my bed *WHHHOOOOO-TA-DOOOO*! Cassie woke up sure thing I told her it was just Dad but she was scared. Mom yelled for Dad to stop it and Dad said no he wouldn't stop that he was drunk that he wanted everyone awake."

"JAKE!"

Huh?

I hear people snickering, see kids' hands up to their mouths.

I feel the blood rush to my face.

"I'm not sure this has anything to do with what we were talking about," Mr. Wyatt says.

"Yeah," says Andy. "What's your drunk dad got to do with the story?"

"Andy, mind your own business," Mr. Wyatt says.

The fire under my skin makes drops of sweat pop up on my forehead. I wipe them with the back of my hand, think how I might have to pee. I hear the door open, and turn. It's Desiree. "Mrs. Maw wants to know where Jake is."

"Did you forget, Jake?" Mr. Wyatt says.

I look at the clock. It's twenty past. I nod, then get up and go to the door, where Desiree is waiting, hands on hips.

Desiree walks beside me like I'm her prisoner. When we pass the boys' room, I duck in.

"I'm telling," she says from the doorway.

"You better not come in here," I say. "I'm unzipping my zipper!"

She gives a little snort and stomps off.

Even though I don't have to go anymore, I lock

myself inside the end stall, flip the seat cover down, and sit. *Idiot!* I can't believe I told the kazoo story. To the whole class! How far did I get?

Mom: "Stop it! Are you out of your mind?"

Dad: "I'm drunk. So what? I want everyone awake. Where're the kids? Kids! Come out here! I got something to announce!"

That's when Cassie took my hand and we went out into the living room. Dad and Mom were in the kitchen, Mom in her bathrobe. She looked more mad than scared. "You smell like a liquor factory," she said.

Dad swayed, as if the floor had suddenly moved beneath him, and grabbed the back of one of the chairs.

"Liquor-smickor," he said. "You all listen. When I was a boy I played a kazoo and my dad hit it out of my mouth. I was making too much noise, he said. So he slapped it out—hard—and the metal cut a hole in my lip. And I couldn't stop the bleeding. Never played music since. Till tonight.

"Then there I am stopping for cigarettes and what do I see right there on the shelf in front of me? A kazoo! Just like the one I had as a kid. So here: *DA-DA-DA-DAAAA-TA-DAH*."

"That's your announcement?" Mom said, shaking her head.

Dad kept blowing, bending up and down like he was a real trumpet player. At first it was scary, but then it got funny. Cassie was half-hiding behind me, her face looking out to see. She started giggling first. Then I did. Even Mom couldn't help but smile. Dad wasn't even looking at us. He was dancing around the kitchen, his eyes kind of crazy and bulging, hair all rumpled and wet, tooting like his life depended on it.

Finally, he ran out of breath . . . stood there breathing hard, his chest moving up and down. "Oh what the hell!" he said. "Go back to bed." Then he wobbled to the bathroom and let out a tremendous fart before he closed the door.

"I'm sorry you have to see your daddy make a

fool of himself," Mom said. "Let's go, I'll tuck you both in. Just pretend it's a bad dream. It's okay. We all make fools of ourselves sometime or other."

Suddenly I remember where I am. I get up and flush, in case someone's in the room. But there's just me. I spend a long time washing my hands, making the soap into a thick lather. After rinsing, I dry off with a paper towel, and notice my reflection in the mirror. I roll the wet paper towel into a cigar, bring it up to my face, bend down and up and down. Like Dad, blowing and humming spit into the kazoo.

I push out air into the towel . . . hum . . . make my neck muscles stick out.

And there in the mirror, I see Dad. See us both. Dad and me. Blowing like our lives depended on it. Blowing like a couple of idiots.

When I get back to class after LEP, everyone is working, dictionaries on their desks. I hear a few whispers and giggles. I slip into my seat and stuff my book in my desk. Then I get out some paper and start drawing the megabat from my poster at home.

I'm scratching in little lines for the fur when Andy gets up to sharpen his pencil. "Hey, Devon," he whispers from the sharpener. "Guess what this is?" Everyone in our group looks up. Andy starts walking back to his desk, wobbling, his eyes rolling in his head. He lets a little gob of spit slip out of the corner of his mouth.

"Some retard?" Devon says.

"Close," Andy says. "It's Ribbet's drunken old man."

I shoot out of my seat, arms and fists flying, catching Andy by surprise, hitting him all over, knocking him against a desk. My eye bursts with a hundred needle points of pain, my leg buckling at the same time. I can't hear anything, just a big angry silence pounding in my head.

"Stop it!" Mr. Wyatt booms, pulling us apart.

"I'll yank those bat ears right off your head!" Andy yells, blood running from his nose.

My eye feels like it's flooded, my knee throbs.

"To the office, now!" Mr. Wyatt tells Andy.

"Trailer trash!" Andy says as he struts out with a fist held up to his nose.

"Outside," Mr. Wyatt tells me. "By the door. You two have no idea how much trouble you're in."

I try to walk without limping, but I can't.

"Look at his eye," someone says, all concerned.

Outside in the hall I slump against the wall. My chest heaves and the whole right side of my face pulses like there's something under the skin wanting out. But it's not the pain I'm thinking of. I'm thinking how mad Dad's gonna be when he finds out I told family stuff in school.

Chapter Twelve

THE PRINCIPAL'S OFFICE has a display of second graders' work on the walls. Cassie's paper is easy to pick out 'cause she always writes big. *If I were in charge of the world there wood be no yelling and toilets wood flush themselfs.*

"I hope you don't think this is funny," Mrs. Beck says. She's already talked to Andy. Now it's my turn.

"No, not funny," I say.

I can't help wondering if Luke has been to the principal's office at his school . . . if there's an amazing fact about principals I should know.

"So tell me what happened. All of it."

When I'm finished she says, "Jake, you don't think fighting solves problems, do you?"

I think of Mom and Dad. "No."

"Attacking another student is a serious infraction. We want our school to be a safe place for all students—"

"I won't do it again," I say, hoping she'll just make me miss recess for a week. "And I'll apologize to Andy too."

"That would be only appropriate," she says. "But it won't get you off the hook. There are consequences to our actions. You will have two days of in-house suspension. Andy will have one day for saying what he did."

I lower my head and hope it's just about over.

"And I have to call your parents."

"What? Why?"

"Because that's the way it's done. Parents must be informed when their child is involved in physical violence or when suspension is involved."

She reaches for the phone.

"They're not home. They work."

She thumbs the big roll of cards on her desk. "Where does your father work?"

"All over. He works for a painting crew."

"And your mom?"

"At the 7-Eleven."

"Which one?

"I'm not sure."

She looks at me. "Are you going to start lying too?"

Mrs. Peterson, the secretary, comes in with the store's phone number. Mrs. Beck dials and tells Mom what happened. "That's right . . . the other boy said something disparaging about Jake's father—I'll let Jake tell you the exact details—and Jake . . ."

When she's done explaining, she hands me the phone.

"A fight, Jake? A fight! In the classroom! What's gotten into you?"

"It wasn't my fault. I mean, I did it, but—you don't know."

"What don't I know?"

I look up to see Mrs. Beck writing notes on a big yellow pad.

"Nothing," I say. "I'm sorry."

"Jesus, Jake." Her voice catches.

"What?"

"It's just bad timing, is all. Your father called earlier. He's finished with the paint crew. He got fired this morning."

I pick up Cassie at her room after school. "How come your face has an *owie*?" she wants to know.

"Never mind," I say. "But Mom's gonna be mad 'cause I got in trouble. Dad might be in a bad mood too. He lost his job today."

"That's good," she says. "Dad hates his job. Remember? . . . He said it's a shi—" She clamps a hand to her mouth. "Remember?"

"It's *not* good," I say. "So don't even mention it. And you can't say nothing about me getting in trouble, either. You got to be 'specially good tonight."

"Okay," she says, her voice suddenly small. "Will Dad get another job?"

" 'Course he will. He always does."

When we get home, I tell Cassie to watch TV while I go see Mrs. Pittmon and clean up after the cats. I change in the shed first, then run over and grab the mail sticking out of her box. "What . . . more junk?" she says when I hand her the stack.

She looks quickly through the letters, and laughs. "Look!" She holds out one of the envelopes for me to read. The name typed over the address says *Nina Pittmon*.

"The cat?" I say. "Nina gets mail?"

"No! Although she's smart enough to. No. . . . I use the name sometimes. Gives me a hoot to see it there. Better than Dolores, don't you think? Imagine a mother naming her baby Dolores. Always hated that name."

I clean up the litter box. Nina and Otto each pick one of my legs to rub against as I refill their water and pour fresh food into their bowls.

"What'd you do to your eye?" Mrs. P. says when I come out of The Bead Room.

"Just something at school," I say.

"Not at home?"

"No. Really. It happened at school."

"Let me guess . . . and you don't want to talk about it?"

I nod.

"Come Friday, I'll probably need help reaching some things on the closet shelves for the yard sale."

"I can do that."

"Good. And you can also talk to me—if you ever need to. About home. School. Whatever. You know that, right?"

"Yep," I say, but after what happened today I don't plan on talking to anybody outside the family about anything. Ever.

Mom comes home from work with a package of hot dogs for supper. "Let me look at you. Not too bad. Does it hurt?"

I shake my head.

"We'll talk later. Help me get started here."

When the hot dogs and mac 'n' cheese are ready, Mom says, "I have no idea where your father is. We'd better start without him." Halfway through supper she gives out a moan and her eyes water like she's gonna cry. She stops herself before the tears can spill over. I suddenly recall one of Luke's amazing facts, the one about astronauts . . . how astronauts can't cry in space because there's no gravity.

"I don't know what we're gonna do," Mom says. "My check will hardly pay the groceries."

"Dad'll find another job," Cassie says. "He always does."

"You're right. He does. He cares about you kids, no matter how mad he gets sometimes." I wait for her to say something about what happened in school but she doesn't.

After supper, we move to the living room. Cassie works on a page of math homework. I take out the drawings I started. Mrs. Maw found me a book with bat skeletons in it, and I'm sketching the bones.

Mom is watching a movie on TV about a woman who got hit on the head and can't remember where she lives. But she keeps looking at the clock. I'm thinking about Dad too, wondering where he is . . . glad when each passing car isn't his. Maybe he won't come home at all. Maybe he's in the car driving and he'll just keep driving. Maybe he'll drive all the way to another state and forget where he lives like the lady in the movie.

I press down hard on the pencil to push away the thought. It's not the first time I've thought about Dad going away and never coming back. Usually it happens when I'm mad. But I'm not mad now. Just scared. Scared that he's been drinking. Scared what he'll say when he finds out about what I told at school. I picture Dad and me and Cassie and Mom together. Laughing. Like the Oaks Park photo on the kitchen wall.

Dad still isn't home when it's time for Cassie to go to bed.

"Come with me, Jake," she says, wanting me to give up the extra half hour I get to stay up.

"No," Mom says. "You go ahead. . . . I need to talk to Jake."

Cassie starts to argue, but I give her a look and she changes her mind.

Mom waits a few minutes after Cassie goes to bed, then pats the sofa for me to join her. She pulls me around so we're facing, puts one finger to her lips and points to the bedroom with the other.

"I'm not gonna tell your father about what happened in school today," she says, almost whispering.

"You're not?"

"No . . . it'll just be one more thing. We've got bigger things to worry about right now. But I need to know what happened. The truth."

My eyes won't stay still as I tell. They keep moving, my gaze jumping from my hands to the walls to the TV to Mom and back again. I tell everything except the part of me and Dad playing kazoos together in the bathroom mirror. It's like a dam breaks behind my eyes when I finish. Then I'm sobbing. Quiet sobs, 'cause I don't want Cassie to hear.

Mom's eyes brim over. She pulls me close, wrapping me in her arms. I clasp back. "Go ahead, get it out," she says as we rock together, back and forth, like swimmers bobbing in water.

When my chest stops heaving, I lift my head from her shoulder and wipe the wet from my face. "I shouldn't have told the kazoo story," I say.

She nods. "It's a matter of family pride. We've got to have *some* family pride." She looks around when she says this, as if the house with our few pieces of furniture and sloping floors would never be enough for a family to be proud of.

"It slipped out, Mom. . . . Honest."

"I believe you."

"And when Andy said what he did, I kinda went crazy."

"He should keep his nose out of other people's business. But people say hurtful things to you all through life. Look at me. I'm heavy now, but I wasn't growing up. I was thin as a bean. The kids in school still found things about me to make fun of. They called me 'Dustmop' because my mother cleaned other people's houses. You can't fight everyone who calls you or someone in your family a name."

I'm wondering if Dad got called names when he was a kid—if people called him "Shorty" or made fun of his teeth—when Mom says, "I'm the one who's sorry, Jake."

"You? For what?"

"For the way things are . . . the way things have become. For what you and Cassie have had to go through lately with your father and me at each other's throats every other minute."

"It hasn't been that bad," I say.

She shakes her head, like she knows what I said is a lie.

"Mom?"

"Hmm?"

"Dad's not a drunk, is he?"

"He drinks too much. He keeps promising to cut down or stop. But I've been waiting a long time now. Maybe long enough."

Suddenly the bedroom door opens and there's Cassie, in her pajamas, eyes slitted against the light, one of Thumper's paws pinched between her fingers.

"Daddy's not a drunk man," she says.

"Of course not, baby," Mom says. "Come here."

Cassie moves to the sofa, and Mom gives her a kiss on the forehead and straightens her hair. "Look at you. You can hardly hold your head up. Let's go back and I'll tuck you in."

"Is Jake coming?"

"I'm not ready yet," I say, 'cause I want to stay up with Mom a little longer. "I need to finish this drawing first."

Cassie takes another look around the room. "Daddy's not home," she says.

"He'll be here soon," Mom tells her. "Come on."

I bet Dad doesn't know that bats have thumbs and fingers. I draw in the little thumb bones that stick out from the middle of each arm, and think about showing the sketch to Dad when it's finished.

Mom comes back from the bedroom in no time. "She's fine," she says when I look up. "Fell back asleep almost as soon as her head hit the pillow. Prob'ly won't even remember she was up tonight."

My stomach flip-flops when I hear the car and see the lights sway past the side window.

Mom's jaw tightens. "Go on—go to bed."

I picture myself running into the bedroom and closing the door . . . hopping under the covers. But I don't. I don't want to leave Mom alone.

The car door slams. Mom turns up the volume on the TV. I jump down to the floor, pick up my pencil, and start shading in wing bones.

"I'm way late," Dad says right away. "But it couldn't be helped."

The churning in my stomach slows. He sounds happy instead of sad.

"I met Ernie down at the club. He says the outfit he works for is looking for a carpenter. He'll put in a good word for me. I'm gonna go in and fill out an application first thing tomorrow."

"You could've called," Mom says without looking away from the TV. "It took you *all* day to find out there's a job opening?"

"We played some cards. Then watched the game on TV. I get a few hours off for a change . . . don't start."

"Jake, what did I tell you?" Mom says.

"Hey, son," Dad says.

"Hey, Dad," I say to the floor, picking up my stuff. "'Night, Dad," I say, a pretend chuckle in my voice—like saying *Hey, Dad . . . 'Night, Dad* is a joke I'm telling. I hold the book up so he won't notice the red around my eye and head for the bedroom, glad when he doesn't call me back for a hug.

Cassie's sleeping, her mouth open a little. I lie in bed like one of Luke's dolphins, with one eye open, waiting for Mom and Dad to go at it. If they do I'll wake Cassie and we'll climb out the window and go to Dragon's Nest. We'll bring blankets and Cassie can take Thumper. Out in the night, we can listen for crickets. "Soon as we hear the Cricket Choir," I'll tell Cassie, "we'll know it's safe to go back inside."

I tune my bat ears toward the living room.

"I'd had it up to here. I finally told that a-hole what I thought of him. It felt good."

"I'm glad you felt good. And what're we supposed to do for money? It's always about you, isn't it?"

"I'll take care of it. I *am* taking care of it."

"Just forget it for tonight. I'm tired. Tired of everything."

Then the TV goes off, and they move to the other end of the house, making the sounds people make when they get ready for bed.

When I wake up, the window is full of gray morning light and Cassie's sniffling.

"What's wrong?"

"I'm all wet, Jake."

"What?"

"I wet the bed."

"Geez," I say. Cassie hasn't wet the bed in a long time. We all thought she was over it. "Better get cleaned up," I say. "We'll take off the sheets and wait till later to tell Mom."

"I don't want Dad to know," Cassie says. "He'll take Thumper away."

I can smell the pee now, drifting over to my side of the room. I get up and pull on my jeans, then open the window to air the place out. Cassie doesn't want me to see. She gets up quickly, pulls a fresh pair of underwear from her drawer, and carries her shorts and shirt into the closet, leaving the door ajar so she can see.

The last time Cassie wet the bed was right before Christmas. Mom said she was just too excited about Santa coming. Dad said if Cassie couldn't get up and go to the bathroom in the night like everyone else, he'd have to take Thumper away, 'cause no rabbit wants to sleep in a pee bed.

I've got the wet sheets and pajamas gathered into a ball for washing. Cassie comes out of the closet all dressed. She's stopped crying, but her eyes are still red. I make a crazy face at her, hoping she'll laugh. But she doesn't.

Chapter Thirteen

*I*N-HOUSE SUSPENSION **means you get to sit at a desk in
the dark hall that separates the main office from
Mrs. Beck's office. For the first day I'm at one end of
the hall, and Andy's at the other. The second day I
have the whole dark hall to myself.

Mrs. Maw comes to my desk early the second
morning with four E-R books. "Ah-ha," she says.
"Thought you could get away from me. Well, when
you're done with that math you might as well
get some reading in too. These four books are on
discs. Here. . . ." She sets up a CD player with an

extension cord to the nearest outlet, then plugs in a set of headphones. "Listen to each book two or three times . . . write down every word that's hard for you." She hands me my LEP journal and waits.

"This is where you're supposed to say 'Will do, Mrs. Maw. What a great idea! Sure. Sounds fun!'"

It's hard not to smile. As soon as she leaves, I dump my math book on the floor and spend the rest of the day reading and listening.

Dad's home when Cassie and I get back from school. He's on the little patio, cleaning up the grill. There's a half-full bottle of beer on the concrete beside him. The garage door is open, and Dad's toolbox is out. Some tools and other things from the garage have been stacked to one side.

"Mom wants you two to decide on what toys you're willing to sell at the yard sale Saturday," Dad says. "We'll put them in the garage. You kids can tag them."

"I've got to remind Mrs. Pittmon to get her stuff ready too," I say.

"Well, hop to it," he says. "What happened to your face?"

"I ran into the goalpost at school," I say, my lie well planned.

"You couldn't find anything softer to hit?"

Cassie looks confused. She's about to say something when I grab her hand, "Come on . . . we got a job to do."

Luke calls me that night. He says he already misses the summer and swimming. "My teacher is the pits," he says. "We can't talk or nothing. And we have to stay in straight lines no matter where we go."

I tell him it's pretty much the same in my school.

"I tried to eat upside down like a flamingo," he says. "I don't recommend it. You gotta take small bites and you're never sure if the food's gonna make it down or come barging back. I've got a bunch of new facts, though. Maybe you can come over Saturday."

"Can't. We're having a yard sale. Hey . . . maybe you could come over and help us with the sale."

"Could I sell some stuff?"

"Sure. Why not?"

"I'll ask my mom," he says. "You ask yours. I'll call you tomorrow. Guess what? I found out bats always turn left when they come out of a cave."

"What?"

"They never exit a cave and turn right, always left."

"How come?"

"I don't know for sure. I haven't got that far yet."

"I'm drawing bat skeletons," I say.

"How many bones do they have?"

"I don't know. Haven't got that far yet."

On Friday I get to go back to class. Mr. Wyatt must have given a speech or something, because everyone is especially nice.

"I'll help you catch up in math," Michelle says. "We can work on it at recess."

"Oooh," Devon says. "Kissy-kissy!"

"Don't be such a baby," Michelle says.

He puts his thumb in his mouth. "But I am a baby."

"No, you're not," Joanna says. "You're a pea-brain posing as one."

My desk has been moved, so that Devon is between me and Andy. I remember what Mom said . . . to be on my toes . . . that Andy might say something just to get me in trouble again. "He knows how to push your buttons. Don't fall into his trap."

But Andy doesn't try to trap me. He's just his usual jerky self. "What do you call a four-hundred-pound teacher named Fatso?" he asks our group when Mr. Wyatt turns his back. We all shrug. "Mr. Fatso!" he says, his train-track braces gleaming.

On my way to LEP, I stop at the desk in the office hall and pick up the books and CD player. "Where's your list of words?" Mrs. Maw asks when I get to class.

"I didn't write any," I say. "It was easy with the discs. You think I could take the tests?"

"Sure you don't want to read the books with me one more time?"

I shake my head and hurry to one of the computers. I call up each book and take my time on each question. "You better check to see how I did," I say when I've finished. But I already know. I missed two. Two out of twenty.

"Alleluia!" Mrs. Maw says when she sees my results. "I think we're on to something here, Jake." She gives me a high five. "Way to go!"

I keep checking the clock all afternoon. Waiting for dismissal. Cassie and I have lots to do to get ready for the yard sale. Mom found a few more things that need stickers and prices. And Kool-Aid. We have to make two jugs of Kool-Aid for selling. Mom checked the weather report this morning and it's supposed to be really hot tomorrow. That's what gave us the idea for Kool-Aid. The best thing is that Luke's coming over. I feel like a cartoon elephant and picture myself raising my trunk and blasting a trumpet call.

Chapter Fourteen

*I*N THE END Cassie can't part with any of her dolls. She puts green stickers on an old Candy Land game, some stuffed animals, a box of broken jewelry, and three half-filled cans of Play-Doh. I'm getting rid of a Mousetrap game with missing pieces, some old Lord of the Rings cards, two GI Joes, and a stack of Disney comics. Mom's gone through our clothes with us, and has taken whatever doesn't fit anymore.

"I still think you're all crazy," Dad says. But he's set aside some tools, three pairs of paint-spattered coveralls, and a set of car tires.

Mrs. Pittmon has a wheelbarrow full of plants. She also has a box of pottery and two boxes of blankets and sheets.

I help Dad carry sawhorses and two large pieces of plywood to the front yard. We make a long table and use the stepladder to run a clothesline between the two trees. It takes a while, but we get it done. When we're finished, Dad rubs the top of my head and squeezes my shoulder. "Thanks, buddy," he says.

Hearing him say that reminds me of when he drove the refrigerator truck for Garden Fine Produce. Sometimes, if there was a day off school and Dad was scheduled for the long drive to Olympia, he'd take me with him. He'd drive the truck right to the house to pick me up. Mom complained it wasn't legal, me riding with him like that during work. But Dad said, "Who's gonna know? Besides, Jake is good company."

It was fun. Halfway up I-5 we'd exit and stop for burgers and shakes at Babe's Café. There was a giant statue of Babe, the big blue ox, out front. When we reached our drop-off point in Olympia, there'd be guys there to unload the boxes of vegetables. Once, Dad gave me a ride on one of the forklifts. I got to raise and lower the big fork and feel the power of it. After driving back, he'd drop me off at home before returning the truck. "Thanks, buddy," he always said before I jumped out.

Dad quit Garden Fine Produce when he didn't get the manager job he thought should have been his. The guy who got it had gone to college. "Which is why you kids need to do well at school," Mom told Cassie and me at the time. "And not be a dumb fool like your old man," Dad said.

I was only in third grade then. But I remember feeling sad to hear Dad call himself a dumb fool.

The sun is already pouring in the window when I wake up the next morning. After a quick breakfast I start hauling everything from the house and garage out to the front.

Mrs. P. comes wheeling up to our yard with a plastic bag of cookies. "We'll need to keep up our strength," she says with a smile.

Dad's already decided he's not staying. "I don't need to see people stick up their noses at us," he says. He's going to run errands and try to catch up with Ernie to see if there's any news about the carpenter job.

"Take whatever you can get for the tires," he tells Mom. "The tools should go for what they're priced." He looks over the long table of for-sale stuff. "Looks like we'll all be on Easy Street after today."

"Go away, Eeyore," Mom says. But she's smiling. "You just might be surprised."

People start coming even before everything is set out. They don't seem very impressed. After an hour the money tray has only a few dollars and quarters in it. Then Mrs. Gilliam comes with Luke and his stuff.

"Here," Mrs. Gilliam tells Mom. "Put these with the rest of your clothes. I don't want any money for them. If they don't sell you can give them to Goodwill."

"Only take a minute for me to tag them," Mom says.

Mrs. Gilliam waves her hand. "Don't be silly . . . really . . . no big deal."

"Are you rich yet?" Luke asks me.

"I got more than I started with," I say, glad he's here.

We set out Luke's things. He's got a bunch of board games, a Twister game, and a whole box of Transformers and action figures.

The Kool-Aid is the biggest seller. That and the clothes. After another hour, I'm just over four dollars. Luke's up to eight. Cassie keeps jingling handfuls of quarters from the Kool-Aid, her forehead dotted with sweat.

When no customers are around, Luke tries to teach Mrs. P. how to work one of the Transformers. Mrs. P. tries, but it's too complicated for her. "Who do you think I am, Einstein?" she says.

For lunch we have the sandwiches that Mom made last night. Plus cookies and Kool-Aid. Luke wants to tell me the amazing facts he's discovered since the last time we saw each other. I tell him to wait, that I've got something to show him.

"Cassie, you watch our stuff, okay?"

"Where you goin'?"

"Never mind. We won't be long. When we come back, we'll give you a break."

"I'm tired too," she says.

"Here," Luke says. "You can have these three Transformers right here. You can sell them and keep the money, or just play with them."

"Really?"

"Really."

I lead Luke back behind the garage.

"What?" he says.

"Wanna show you what I made."

We come to the hedge. "Whaddya see?" I ask.

"Where?"

"There."

"I see a hedge. A big one."

"Anything else?"

He squints at the hedge. "If I look real hard, I see something, but I can't tell what it is."

"That's Mrs. Pittmon's house," I say. "Up front here you can just make it out . . . the branches aren't as thick as farther down."

I walk on, and Luke follows me along the hedge. "Keep looking," I say.

"What am I looking for?"

"You'll see."

We come to the end of the yard, where the hedge meets a falling-over fence that separates our backyard from the people on the other street.

I move to the hedge and lift away first one layer, then another layer of branches. "Go ahead," I say, as if holding open a door. "Go in."

Luke steps over a few twigs low to the ground and moves his head and shoulders into the hedge.

"All the way," I say.

He steps all the way in, and I follow, letting the

branches swing back behind me, the door closing, the two of us scrunched together in the hollowed-out room.

"Wow," Luke says, "you'd never know it was in here."

"I used Dad's pruning saw," I say. "And Mom's clippers. I hid all the stuff I cut on Mrs. Pittmon's side so Dad and Mom can't tell. . . . Sit down."

He settles onto Cassie's flat stone. "Cool," he says.

"Even when it rains, it's dry in here," I say. "Me and Cassie tested it. 'Course Mom and Dad don't know. Just Cassie and me, and now you. . . . So tell me your new bat info."

"Oh, I got bat stuff," he says. "But you gotta hear this first. You know frogs, right? Well, they can throw up just like people. 'Cept it's different. The frog throws up its *stomach*! The stomach dangles from the frog's mouth. Then it uses its little arms in front to dig out the stuff in its stomach and—"

"And what?"

"And swallows the stomach back down!"

"No way," I say.

"Way," he says. "And this one: You can't sneeze with your eyes open. No one can. It's impossible. I already made two dollars betting guys at my school. I used black pepper to make them sneeze."

I flick off an ant that has climbed onto my leg, thinking how I'll fool Andy and Devon and the other guys with the sneeze thing. They think they know everything. Bet they don't know this.

"And listen . . . you know who's got the largest eyes in the world, dontcha?"

"Nope."

"The giant squid. Their eyes are awesome. And it's sea horse fathers, not the mothers, who have the babies!"

"Jake?"

Luke freezes, his eyes ballooning like he's trying to imitate a giant squid. I must look the same, hearing just a voice talking out there past the branches. Then I hear my name again. And I know.

"Cassie!" I whisper. "Go away."

"Why? I want to play too."

We can just see pieces of her shorts and shirt through the webbing of leaves and branches. She's pressing up against the hedge, an arm's length away.

"This is boy stuff," I say. "Now go away before Dad or Mom sees you. . . . There's only room for two anyway, you know that."

"But you said Dragon's Nest was our place. Just ours. We weren't supposed to show anyone. We crossed on it."

"It *is* half yours. But Luke isn't just anyone. He's one of us."

She reaches her hands slowly into the green, fingers worming their way. I pinch them. Hard. She yowls. Whatever magic Luke and I had being in Dragon's Nest is over.

"Come on, Luke," I say, disgusted. "Geez, Cassie, you have to ruin everything."

I lead the way, bending and squirming through to the outside where Cassie is pouting.

"Why ya stopping?" she says.

"'Cause of you. Butting in."

She looks hurt. But I don't care. I'm tired of having a baby sister following me everywhere. "Go ahead, go in there and play by yourself. We've got other things to do."

Luke and I walk back to the house. I know Cassie's still standing there by the hedge. Being sad. But I don't look back.

Chapter Fifteen

*M*OM CALLS OFF the sale at four o'clock. "We've done as much as we're going to," she says. "Got enough here for new shoes for you and Cassie, and then some," she tells me. "Wait till I show your father. He thinks he's so smart."

Luke and I help Mrs. P. back to her house. Nina and Otto are there at the door, yawning.

"Thanks," Mrs. P. says. "Time for my nap. It was fun. . . . Good talking with your mom."

Luke and I take what's left from the sale back to the garage. Then I show him my bat skeleton drawings and he shows me his drawing of a frog throwing up. We're tossing around a tennis ball out back when Dad gets home.

The night starts great. Dad cooks out on the grill, those long skinny hot dogs. I can eat three of them. We have chips and salad too, eating on the little cement patio with the weeds poking through the cracks. Mom, Dad, Luke, me, and Cassie sit around the picnic table that's propped up on one end by concrete blocks. It's still pretty hot, but at least the table's in the shade.

Luke and I keep giggling, remembering his latest facts. Cassie and Mom try to find out what we're laughing about. But their questions just make us laugh harder. Whenever I say *frog,* Luke moves his hand up his chest to his mouth, like his stomach's coming out. He says, "Grandma, what big eyes you have," and I say, "What do you expect, squiddo!"

"Sea horse babies!" I say.

"Mama!" he says. "I mean, *Papa* . . . I mean—" He sputters out some hot dog with his laugh.

Dad and Mom shake their heads. Cassie tries to get in on the fun by opening her mouth when it's full of food.

"Uh-uh," Dad tells her. "Not polite, you know that."

"Mrs. Pittmon sure likes to talk," Mom says.

"I can't believe someone wanted those tires," Dad says.

Finally Mom says it's time to clean up, and we all start to help. Except Dad. He stays seated, looking as if he's trying to figure something out, his gaze moving from the patio to the house, then to the garage, the broken-down shed . . . the yard.

Luke says he needs to use the bathroom. I take some dirty plates and walk with him inside. It's dark in the kitchen. I can see Mom and Dad and Cassie through the screened window over the sink.

"You didn't even touch your salad," Mom tells Cassie.

"You know . . . this place is a dump," Dad says.

"Oh, please, don't start on this one again."

"No, I mean it. Just looking at it with an objective eye. I mean, sitting here like this, on a Saturday night in September . . . just pretending to be a stranger and looking around, seeing stuff for the first time . . . this place is a real dump."

"End it, okay? Jake's got Luke over. And I'm sick of hea.ing about how much of a failure I am."

"Not just you," Dad says.

"Oh, I see . . . we're gonna start feeling sorry for ourselves again."

She picks up the pitcher of Kool-Aid and storms into the house. Cassie follows her, scurrying like a duckling who wants to keep its mom in sight.

I hear the toilet flush. Luke comes out. "I'd better call for my mom to come get me," he says.

"But we might go for ice cream," Cassie says.

"Mom said to call her right after we eat."

I know he doesn't have to rush home . . . know he'd come for ice cream if he hadn't heard Mom and Dad talking like that. I want to shout *Look what you did!* to Mom and Dad. *You can't be with each other for one minute without making someone scared.*

"I'll drop you off," Dad says. "I need to stop at the store."

"Now there's a surprise," Mom says, half under her breath.

"What?"

"Nothing. Go. You get to leave whenever you want. I'm the one who has to stay in your so-called dump."

"I'm not gonna listen to this," Dad says. "Come on, Luke."

I walk Luke to the car and say good-bye. He says maybe next weekend I can come and spend the night at his house.

"Maybe," I say. "That'd be good."

Then Dad and Luke drive away and Mom starts the water for dishes. She flicks the radio on to a country station and turns it up loud.

"Did Dad get to see Ernie?" I ask over the music.

She shuts off the water and turns to look at me.

"The job's been filled if that's what you're asking. But, you needn't worry over it. Something else'll come up."

"Can we go for ice cream when Dad comes back?" Cassie asks.

"I'm not sure Dad will be coming back right away," Mom says. "Maybe . . . if he does. If he doesn't, the three of us can go for a walk. It's a beautiful night. I'm tired of your father taking the fun out of things. We can make a batch of popcorn and watch TV when we get back."

"Can I stay up late?"

"We'll see."

Dad does come back, with Kit Kats for me and Cassie. There's also a quart of beer in the bag. He cracks the top open and fills a glass.

"Hot," he says. "What's this I hear about going for ice cream?"

"Can we, Daddy?" Cassie asks.

Dad finishes his drink and puts the bottle in the

fridge. Mom isn't through with the dishes yet. "Come on," Dad says. "Just leave it. We'll take a drive to cool down. Get out of the city."

The car has been soaking in the sun. Dad starts the engine. "Turn on the air conditioning full blast!" he says.

Cassie giggles as we all roll down our windows as far as they'll go.

Dad backs into the street and takes off, making the tires squeal like he does from time to time "just to let everyone know we're here."

"Do you have to peel out like that?" Mom says.

"Why, what's wrong with it?"

"It's immature. Something a sixteen-year-old would do to impress his girlfriend. I'm not sixteen, in case you haven't noticed."

Dad looks her over. "I can see that. . . . Never bothered you before."

"Well, it's embarrassing."

"I'm embarrassing to you?"

I'd seen enough of Mom and Dad's fights to

know that some start right away, with a *whoosh,* like when you put a match to the barbecue after you've poured a lot of starter fluid on it. Other times you're not even sure there's any burning at all going on under the charcoal.

Mom and Dad don't say anything for a long time. But the fire must be smoldering because once we get away from the city Dad says, "Maybe I should list the things about *you* that embarrass *me.*"

"I didn't say *you* embarrassed me," Mom says. "I said *it* embarrassed me."

"Same thing."

"Maybe you should just drive."

"Jake, how come I don't remember marrying such a bossy woman?" Dad says, looking back at me in the mirror.

I don't know what to say, so I pretend I need to itch an old mosquito bite on my leg, my stomach going floaty.

Dad doesn't ask the question again. There's hardly any traffic now that we've reached the country. We used to drive out to the country a lot when Cassie and I were little, looking for the perfect house. It was a game Mom and Dad liked to play. Dad would drive and Mom would point out which roads to turn down. Then we'd all look at the houses and farms. The idea was to find a place that was "perfect"—the perfect house and property we'd buy if we had the money. Mom and Dad were fussy about it too. The perfect house couldn't be too close to the road. There had to be trees for shade. A workshop for Dad. And a pond for me and Cassie.

"Are we going to look at houses?" Cassie says now.

I put my finger to my lips to tell her to be quiet.

"No," Dad says. "No houses this time."

The road goes up and up until it comes to another road called Skyline. From Skyline you can see everything for miles. "We're at the top of the world," Cassie says, letting the wind blow her hair around.

"You always need to be in control of things," Dad

says, as if he and Mom have been talking all this time.

"Oh for crying out loud," Mom says. "Can't you take even the tiniest criticism?"

Then quiet again, except for the rush of air. When Dad slows down for curves I prick up my bat ears, listening hard, hoping to hear crickets.

Dad goes fast down a long straight stretch, and I stick my face into the wind. The air tickles, crashes, streams over the stubby hairs of my head like quick-moving water.

We pull into Esther's Country Store when it's almost dark. A group of soccer players in purple uniform shirts are crowded around the back of a van near the order window. Other families are eating their ice cream in their cars. Two of the cars have the same radio station on, the music echoing out the open windows. Everyone looks glad to be out eating ice cream on such a nice night.

I have chocolate and Cassie has bubble gum. Mom has a baby scoop of maple walnut in a cup 'cause she's back on her diet. Dad has a Coke and smokes a cigarette. We sit at one of the picnic tables on the grass where the parking lot ends.

"Jake, look!" Cassie says. She points to where the grass meets a big open field. At the edge of the grass is a baby rabbit, its white tail twitching. We take long, slow-motion steps to see how close we can get. The rabbit lifts its head, takes another bite of grass, then scoots on three hops into the brush of the field. When we reach the place where the rabbit was eating, I tell Cassie to look up. There must be a zillion stars out.

"We can't see these stars from our house," Cassie says.

"They're up there," I say. "But the lights from the city get in the way."

We lick our cones and watch the sky.

"Where's the Cricket Choir, Jake?"

I listen.

"They're prob'ly taking a rest," I say.

There must be a lot of stuff in the air over the

field 'cause Cassie starts coughing. Then back at the picnic table Mom and Dad are yelling—right there in the open, in front of everyone.

"The same song and dance, over and over. . . . Take the whole damn wallet, you take everything else!"

Cassie grabs my arm, her ice cream in need of licking.

The people in their cars are looking now. At the picnic table. At Mom and Dad. That's when Dad gets into the car and orders us all in. He pulls out of the parking lot so fast there's a cloud of dust left behind, a monster cloud gobbling up Esther's Country Store.

Dad drives really fast. So fast that Cassie looks at me with fear in her eyes. I want to tell Dad to knock it off. Cassie has forgotten all about her ice cream, the scoops wobbling in the cone that shakes with her coughing.

"Rob, stop it!"

Dad makes the car go even faster, the car cresting

the top of the hill that leads a back way into town. The road is steep and narrow, with a bridge at the bottom that crosses a creek.

"I'll put us all down!" Dad says, the darkness whirring past.

"No, Dad!" I say. "Please go slow!"

Mom screams Dad's name again and hits him hard in the shoulder. The car swerves, spins. Suddenly everything goes quiet. It's as if the whole world has to freeze to see if we'll go tumbling over or slide off the road . . . if there are going to be sirens.

The brakes screech, and I'm jerked forward, the seat belt ripping into my stomach. We're stopped in the middle of the bridge, facing the creek and woods. The creek looks surprised by the car's lights. Cassie's crying, soft sobs. Our ice-cream cones have been flung from our hands. They lie on the floor, melting into the dirty mats.

"SEE!" Dad shouts. "See what you make me do!"

He turns the car around so it's facing the road

again. Then the car moves forward, real slow, like it's scared too.

We drive a long way in silence. Mom and Dad keep looking straight ahead. Cassie and I study our melting cones through the on-again, off-again reflections of passing cars.

"It's okay, kids," Mom turns and says when we reach town.

"They're fine," Dad says. "They're not as damned delicate as you think."

Mom reaches back to touch Cassie's face, wiping some of the dirty wet away with her thumb. And when I look up I see Dad's eyes in the mirror looking at me.

"You're not crying, are you, Jake?"

I drop my gaze to the hair on the back of his head, feel a tear snake down one side of my face.

"I don't know what the hell you're crying for. We're all fine, aren't we?"

I nod.

"What?"

"Yes," I say.

"Leave him alone," Mom says.

Cassie sniffles and coughs, sniffles and coughs.

I wish more than anything that we'd never gone for ice cream.

Dad steers the car into the driveway and steps hard on the brake. "Home, sweet home!" he says.

Mom rushes to open Cassie's door. I get out my side—and hear my name called. *Jake? Jake!* It takes a second to figure where it's coming from.

"It's Mrs. P.," I tell Mom. "I said I'd clean up after the cats. I forgot."

Dad sits unmoving behind the wheel. Mom has Cassie by the hand. "Tell her we're busy and you'll do it tomorrow," she says. "I want you here with us."

I duck around the front of the hedge. Mrs. P. is in her chair on the little front porch. It's dark out, but there's enough light coming through the screen door to see.

"I can't do the cats right now," I say. "We're really busy."

"I'm not worried about the cats," she says, holding up a card. "Here's the recipe your mom and I talked about today. I've got to do things right away or I forget. Nice night, huh? Won't be many more like this. You go for a ride?"

"Yeah," I say, my stomach all snakes again.

I take the card and our eyes meet. I look away, not wanting her to see that I've been crying.

"What's happened? What's the matter?"

"Thanks," I say. "I really need to go."

Dad is tossing out the mats from the backseat as I hurry for the house and Mom and Cassie. Inside, Mom's using a wet towel to wipe the dried bubble gum ice cream from Cassie's face. "You two can forget about brushing your teeth. Just undress and get into bed."

Cassie's down to her underwear when she gasps.

"Mommy!" she says, like she's stepped on a bee. Her mouth is open, her eyes wide with surprise. A creaky wheeze comes from her throat.

Mom runs out to the kitchen and comes back

with a glass of water, and holds the rim to Cassie's lips. Cassie takes a sip, but the water comes back out.

"Jake, get her inhaler!" Mom says.

Dad comes in and says we should hop back in the car and take her to the emergency. "And how do we pay for it?" Mom screams.

My hands are shaking as I hand Mom the inhaler. She puts the mouthpiece in Cassie's mouth. "Breathe, honey . . . come on . . . that's it."

"We should go in," Dad says.

Mom looks at him. "I'll rot in hell before I get back in that car with you."

Dad grabs her arm, his face suddenly pinched and red.

"I'm not afraid of you!" Mom says.

I see the back of Dad's hand come up. Then I hear the sound of it against Mom's face. Her shriek.

"Run!" I tell Cassie. "Run!"

Chapter Sixteen

MOM HAS FALLEN onto Cassie's bed.

"I'm sick of it. Sick of feeling like a loser around you!" Dad yells.

"Dad, please," I say.

"Shut up!" He grabs the lamp on the night table and throws it against the wall. Then sweeps the back of his arm across the top of Cassie's chest of drawers, sending everything to the floor.

"Go ahead," Mom says. "Show your son what kind of man you are."

Dad grabs her and stands her up. Mom slaps at him with her free hand. I lunge, sobbing, at Dad's leg and try to pull him away, the three of us like some weird statue, arms and legs mixed up in one another.

"Don't . . . please . . . don't!" I keep saying.

"THAT'S ENOUGH!" A new voice. Strong and clear.

"STOP IT, I say!"

It's Mrs. Pittmon, her wheelchair full in the doorway.

I crawl on my hands and knees over to her, lay my face in her lap. Dad and Mom disconnect, Mom falling back onto the bed. Then I see colored lights swirling over the walls. And in no time two police officers appear behind Mrs. P. and me.

Dad crumples to his knees. "I didn't mean—"

"Cassie!" Mom cries. "Where's Cassie?"

I run through the house and out the back door into the dark, down the side of the hedge till I hear crying, wheezing. I find the opening and plunge into Dragon's Nest, where Cassie sits small and shivering on her stone.

I put my hands on her shoulders. "It's okay," I say.

"You did good." But her wheezing won't stop. "She's here!" I yell when Mom calls my name from the patio.

The light from the kitchen shows Cassie in her underwear, scratched up from the branches. She's still coughing and wheezing. Mom grabs her up in her arms.

The lady police officer offers to take us to the hospital.

"You better," Mrs. P. says. "Just in case."

"I can take your report there," the officer says. "Officer Lopez will take your husband's."

Chapter Seventeen

*A*LMOST FOUR WEEKS have passed since the yard sale and that night. Halloween is nearly here. This year Cassie's going to be a pirate and wear a beard. She's tired of being a princess. Mom found a nice beard on sale at Walgreens. It's black and long and wavy. Cassie puts it on every night to practice. Luke and I are going to paint our faces and be whatever looks back at us in the mirror.

Cassie's Barbie backpack bobs now as she kicks through fallen leaves on the way home from school. I follow behind, checking out people's jack-o'-lanterns and breathing the crushed-leaf smell.

Inside my pack is the new CD-cassette player Mrs. Maw gave me. "For you and the family," she said. I can't wait to show Mom. Mrs. Maw also gave me a new set of books and discs for the weekend . . . and a package of blank tapes. "Your sister tells me you're a good storyteller," she said. "If you feel like taping yourself, I'd be glad to hear them. Maybe we could type them out. I know you're a good drawer; you could do illustrations. Write a book!"

"I don't know," I said. "I'd probably get all nervous with the tape running."

"Find a quiet place. Can you think of a quiet place?"

The first place that comes to mind is Mrs. P.'s Bead Room. I picture me in the center of the floor talking into the microphone, with Nina and Otto sleeping on top of the little sofa.

None of the kids at school know about Dad. How he had to spend two days in jail. Then when Mom was at work and Cassie and I were at school, he came to get his stuff. He's staying with Ernie in the next town over. He's not allowed to see us. Not for a while yet. Mom says he's seeing some counselor person to work on not getting so mad all the time.

Cassie hasn't had another asthma attack since that night. Mom offered to have Cassie move into her room with her so I could finally have a room of my own. But Cassie and I decided to keep things the same for a little while. She wets the bed now and then, and gets sad when she thinks about not having Dad around. That's when she needs to hear a story. Cassie says Mom's stories aren't as good as mine.

If I end up telling a book about the adventures of Smoke and Bonfire, I'm going to dedicate it to Cassie.

Cassie doesn't think I can see her now, sneaking behind the tree in front of Mrs. Pittmon's. I pretend not to know and keep walking. When I come to the tree, she jumps out and sprays me with leaves. Then I get her back. We're screaming and everything, so at first I don't notice Dad's car. It's halfway down the block, parked on the opposite side of the street.

"Okay—okay!" I say. "You got me enough. You win."

I reach in my pocket and pull out the key that came with the house's new locks and give it to her. "You go ahead. I need to stop in to see about Nina and Otto. You're gonna watch cartoons, right?"

She nods and takes the key, but still has a few leaves in one hand. She jumps up, giggling, and rubs the leaves over my head. "You're in for it next time," I say, flicking off the leaf parts.

I watch her run to the house and go in . . . wait till I know she's turned on the TV, then turn and walk up the street toward the car.

As I get closer, I can hear the car idling, sounding as noisy and out-of-tune as always. I stand just opposite the car, on the other side of the street. Dad waves, his window down, then turns the engine off. Mom would kill me if she knew I was breaking my promise. But it's been almost a month.

"Hey," I say.

"Hey," he says. Then adds, "You don't have to come to the car. You stay right there if you want. I just needed to get a look at you two. This is the first time I've been here. Honest."

Suddenly the bad pictures of that night return. They come back often. The back of Dad's hand rising. The sickening sound as it catches Mom's face. Cassie gasping for air. And me, clutching a leg, holding on for dear life to something that keeps moving away.

"I better stay over here," I say. "I made a promise. . . . But Dad . . . how you doin'?"

"Okay, son. You and Cassie and your mom doing all right?"

"Mom got more hours at work," I say. "Cassie won Star Student of the Week."

I don't mention that Mom laughs a lot more now . . . that she's lost five pounds . . . that the house seems easier to breathe in.

"I got a job. . . . Did that much," he says. "You're

not going to believe this, though. I work for a pipe-laying outfit. We do a lot of sewers." He smiles. "You don't get it, do you?"

"No," I say.

"Sewers? Shitty jobs?"

"Oh, yeah," I say. "I get it. That's a good one."

"Well, I best be going," he says. "Tell Cassie Daddy's trying . . . that Daddy loves her. You too."

"I liked your postcard," I say.

"Not that easy finding a postcard with a bat on it," he says.

"Guess not."

"Take it easy, then."

He starts the engine. I don't know why, but I'm hoping he'll peel out, "just to let everyone know we're here." But he doesn't. A little ways down the block he toots. I wave back.

Mrs. Pittmon calls for me to come help her carry over the supper she's made: meatloaf and baked potatoes covered with cheese sauce. Everything's really good. Mom thanks Mrs. P. over and over, like she usually does. Mrs. P. says what she always says: "Ain't nothing."

It gets dark early now. Cassie and I barely have time to go outside and work on Dragon's Nest. We've been expanding it. We've got three rooms now. One for Cassie, one for me, and a guest room for Luke or Cassie's friends when they come over. I've been thinking that when Cassie's birthday comes around next spring, I'll surprise her and give her all of Dragon's Nest. That way she can have the whole Barbie Club over at the same time. I'll be busy anyway. Luke and I are planning a spring project. We promised to keep it a secret. But I'd better start teaching Mom more good stuff about bats.

"Hey, you two!" Mom calls from the patio. "What about your homework?"

"Coming," I say. "Let's go, Cassie. . . . It's too dark to see what we're cutting."

There's a little more light once we're out of the hedge. Halfway to the house, my ears twitch.

"Listen!"

Cassie stops. "I don't—"

"There!"

Her eyes squinch up. "Oh, yeah."

Crickets. Not a full choir. Just a few end-of-the-season chirps in the empty lot a couple houses away.

"That's good luck, right?" Cassie says.

"Yep," I say.

"Should I think of a wish?"

"Yeah."

I don't know if Cassie has her eyes closed, but I do. I wish for Dad to get better, so maybe he can come home. And for Mom to not get so worried about bills. And—while I'm at it—I wish for a flying dream tonight. 'Cause those are the best. Luke and I both agree. Flying dreams are the best.

About the Author

DAVID GIFALDI is a fifth-grade teacher and the author of several novels for young readers, including *Toby Scudder, Ultimate Warrior* and *Rearranging, And Other Stories*. He is also on the faculty of the MFA in Writing for Children and Young Adults program at Vermont College. He lives in Portland, Oregon.

www.davidgifaldi.com